***

She's a space pirate with vital information. He's a wanted fugitive with enemies hot on his afterburner. Will their unexpected attraction survive escaping a dangerous asteroid mine in time to avert disaster?

Trouble is arising across the galaxy, and space pirate Julke Defjensdytr has vital information for her clan. She's almost given up trying to escape the hidden rogue asteroid mine she's been imprisoned in for over a year. But a new batch of prisoners brings hope in the form of kind and sexy Zade.

Starship crewman and wanted fugitive Zade Lunaso always runs from conflict. Unfortunately, this time it landed him with a one-way ticket to toil in the dangerous mine for the rest of his soon-to-be short life. He'll need all his considerable skills to escape. Not to mention help from the intriguing Julke, and a flock of curious space griffins with secrets of their own.

Their bid to steal the cruel Warden's yacht goes off course when they take a wrong turn and discover a motherload of forgotten ships. But even if they somehow free every prisoner to fly them, the Warden will kill them all to protect the secret of his claim.

The arrival of bigger enemies means trouble has found Zade once again. Can Julke and Zade pull off the unlikeliest escape off a lifetime, or will their luck play out and leave them stranded in the void?

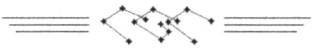

ALSO BY CAROL VAN NATTA

Space Opera - Central Galactic Concordance Series

- Last Ship Off Polaris-G (Novella)
- Overload Flux (Book 1)
- Minder Rising (Book 2)
- Zero Flux (Novella)
- Pico's Crush (Book 3)
- Pet Trade (Novella)
- Jumper's Hope (Book 4)
- Cats of War (Novella)
- Galactic Search and Rescue (Novella)
- Escape from Nova Nine (Novella)
- Spark Transform (Book 5)

Retro Science Fiction Comedy

- Hooray for Holopticon

Paranormal Romance

- Shifter Mate Magic (Ice Age Shifters #1)
- Shift of Destiny (Ice Age Shifters #2)
- Heart of a Dire Wolf (Ice Age Shifters #3)
- Dire Wolf Wanted (Ice Age Shifters #4)
- Shifter's Storm (Ice Age Shifters #5)
- In Graves Below (Magic, New Mexico)

ESCAPE FROM NOVA NINE

A CENTRAL GALACTIC CONCORDANCE
NOVELLA

CAROL VAN NATTA

1

Zade Lunaso hunched, cramming his shoulders into the shadowed corner of a painted metal support pillar, struggling to hide his gasps for air. The lumpy backpack jabbed his kidneys. Under the hood of his winter long coat, sweat dripped down his neck, magnifying the heat rash already prickling on his chest. He swallowed hard against the tickle in his throat that threatened to explode into a coughing fit. Regular use of a starship's creaky treadmill hadn't prepared him for a desperate dodge and dash through the automated cargo loading area of a space station.

Once again, Zade found himself in urgent need of a new job. His soon-to-be-former crew didn't know he'd slipped past their security and off the ship. However, once they did a physical check instead of relying on their tech, they'd come after him. And know where to look, too.

Every station in the galaxy had unofficial areas for in-person hiring. According to his research, Shenyan Surkai Station's spot was the commons area behind tourist shop row and in front of several independent trader company offices. It was his best bet for getting off the station fast.

The adrenaline that fueled his run was no longer helping. He took four slow, deep breaths, imagining he heard a bell tone, visualizing calm, cooling air saturating every cell in his body. With each slow exhale, he eyed the commons area for entrances and exits.

Purposeful people crossed the commons like they were late. Loiterers leaned on pillars or sat on benches, watching the action.

In out-of-the-way stations like Shenyan Surkai, recruiters were likely hoping to fill an unexpected staffing gap. Smart ship crew usually chose high-traffic hubs to look for a new job. Maybe someday he'd be lucky enough to do the same.

Cautiously, he reached out with a feather touch of his empath talent to gauge the mood of the loiterers. Emotions came to him like flavors. A few hints of bitter fear, a few more of acidic anger. Some salty annoyance and minty impatience. The fishy flavor of smug condescension near the open door of the largest trader association. To his right, the over-sweet taste of bliss, possibly the result of a visit to the local chems and alterants shop. Nothing out of the ordinary.

His minder talent for sensing and influencing emotions was a part of him, and he wouldn't give it up if he could, but it closed doors. The Central Galactic Concordance traditional military detested minders and force-transferred them to the Citizen Protection Service. The CPS was still nominally military, but with its own rules. The CGC High Court had struck down minder registration laws decades ago, but far too many of the CGC's five hundred member planets had subtler restrictions woven throughout their statutes. Interstellar trade guilds and associations found many ways to relegate known minders.

That attitude spilled over to less-traveled star lanes. Both indie traders who worked the fringes and freelance jacker crews who hunted commercial ships often shunned minders. Rumors said the secretive pirate clan, who competed with interstellar jackers for juicy slice-and-hauls of fat freighters in deep space, had more minders than nulls. He snorted with momentary amusement. He doubted the clan would openly recruit in CGC territory, no matter how backwater the station. Besides, a stint with the scourge of the galaxy wouldn't add luster to his qualifications record for future job searches.

The elongated hexagon on the back of his left hand vibrated. With casual movements, he read the percomp's holo display. Thank the universe! His earlier anonymous query to the station's official job bank was paying off. An indie trader needed a cargo handler, one of the many shipboard jobs he could do. They were leaving within a few hours, and from a loading bay on the other side of the station from the ship he'd recently exited. To top it off, they claimed to be a minder-friendly outfit.

It sounded too good to be true, until he looked at the pay. Meals, shift-share quarters, and a backend share of the unspecified cargo's sale. Funny how those jobs never seemed to make a profit. No wonder they had to take minders.

Easing out from behind the pillar, he sized up the

recruiters. He ruled out the woman in menacing black with weapons to match. Avoiding conflict topped his life-lessons list. The blissfully chemmed recruiter might not remember anything they promised.

He pushed back the furry winter hood. After a few moments of letting the sweat on his neck evaporate in the station's dry air, he eased into the crowd, headed for the smug pair of indie traders in matching colors. His damp black topknot of hair and the long coat probably made him look like a solo scout or a hothouse noob who hadn't acclimated to cooler ship temperatures. Hopefully, his twenty years of quals would encourage them to take a second look. He'd only taken a few steps when the sulfuric stench of rage brushed the edge of his talent.

He knew it all too well. His former employer, interstellar jacker captain Fazhian.

Quelling the urge to run, he pulled the hood back up and turned right to merge into a clump of fast-walking pedestrians. He only had a small window of time to escape.

Fazhian was dangerous when on a rampage, but prone to tantrums. However, once her anger subsided, her cunning would be back online. She lovingly nurtured grudges. He'd seen her go parsecs out of her way to exact retribution against one of her long list of enemies.

Staying on the station wasn't an option. Concordance foundation law said space stations had to provide breathable air, a liter of water per day, and gravity. Everything else had a price. His funds were tied up, so even if he miraculously eluded the captain and her crew, she'd make farkin' sure to destroy his chances of finding another ship before she left.

A split-second decision took him to the corridor toward the Y-axis dock. If the no-pay cargo handler job checked out, that ship was his best hope. He used his percomp to send his quals to the ping ref in the job listing. With luck, they'd take him before Fazhian poisoned the well. All he needed was a little time to regroup and get back on his new path.

The station's direction markers were clear enough that he didn't need to stop at a kiosk for directions in finding the job listing's docking slot. The giant connector rings in this section looked newer than the one his former ship had docked at. Too bad for his aching legs that the hiring ship was in the farthest slot in this section. He kept his head down as he passed those with open freight airlocks, especially if humans were around to maybe notice him.

He slowed as he got closer, sending out his talent to look for trouble.

What he found instead was two active shielders, who may as well have been black holes as far as emotional broadcasts went. Four other people stood nearby, feeling guarded and hopeful, just like him. He let his feet carry him closer.

A loud tenor voice boomed out, obviously amplified. "Lookin' for somethin', friend?" The language was Standard English. The musical, polyglot accent could have come from any multicultural city.

Zade edged closer, clearing his throat. "Cargo handler job." Just in case, he repeated it in Mandarin, the second most common language in the galaxy. Some outfits clung to old habits, even though the CGC had mandated Standard English as the official language almost two hundred years ago. Speaking Mandarin might make him more employable.

"This be the place." The voice sounded cheerful.

Overhead floating lights grew brighter and defined a soft circle on the hatch-textured floor. A short man strode into the center carrying a tablet. His long, sleeveless vest flapped over nondescript pants and a shorter, long-sleeved tunic. Dark hair coiled tight and close to his head. "Friends, if you'll move closer, I won't have to shout."

Different voice, not amplified.

The others stepped more into the circle. After a moment, Zade did, too.

A light touch with his talent said no one felt worried. Their clothes and luggage suggested indie crew, and maybe a jacker. He tentatively tagged them as two men and two women, but he was a bad judge of such things. Emotions had no gender markers. And with the thousands of body shops on every planet in the galaxy, they could be anything they wanted to be.

The short man tapped his tablet. "Call me Fortezza. Tell me your names and if you got any certs."

Zade pegged it for a nickname, since it meant "fortress" in Italian and shielders like such affectations. Still a black hole as far as his talent could tell. The short man's accent was different from the other voice, but still had multicultural cadence. No jewelry and no visible art on his dark brown skin to hint at origin or affiliation, either.

One of the women fluttered three beringed fingers.

"I'm Robb. Navigator 2-E." Tasteful tattoos on her slender brown neck surrounded the jack interface behind her ear. Her accent hinted at something Slavic as her primary language.

"Jurten. Commtech 4E," said the man in coordinated shades of gray that contrasted with his white skin and pale blond hair.

Zade and the others gave their names, with no certifications to claim.

"Okay. Any of you minders?" He pointed to himself, then aimed a thumb over his shoulder. "We're minders ourselves. Adir and me are shielders. Us and our sister ship just like to know who we'd be traveling with."

The wariness in the group spiked.

"I'm *not* a minder," said the navigator with a forward jut of her jaw. "Will that be a problem?"

"Not unless you refuse to work with minders," replied the short man.

The navigator shrugged. "Not a problem."

He nodded, then looked around the group.

The communications technician crossed his arms, sliding his hands under his armpits. "I'm a filer."

Zade envied the man's ability to remember everything. Wo Zhur, the other woman, admitted to being a fixer and good with ship engines and environmental systems.

Waorani, a broad-faced man with swirling runic patterns on his deep olive skin, said he was a low-level sifter. Another talent Zade appreciated. It'd be nice to know when unshielded people were lying or about to become violent. Not to mention, know when other minders were activating their talent. Zade knew from experience that his was hard to detect, but high-level sifters could sense it, even if they didn't know what it was.

At the short man's questioning look, Zade shrugged one shoulder. "Lunaso. Low-level empath."

The short man moved a few things on his tablet. "Okay, we're green go. Your quals check out, so you're all hired. I'm sending you the contract..." His tablet suddenly went black. He swore. "Cool your jets a sec."

He strode out of the circle toward the large entry lock. "Adir, I need a new tablet. Mine's malfing."

"Again?" the amplified voice boomed. "Garka, get out here and give him yours."

The only warning Zade had of trouble was the sudden look of panic on Waorani's face as he launched himself away from the entry lock.

Pain exploded in Zade's neck. Fire burned his hand. He staggered toward the darkness. Another jolt.

Around him, the others fell, twitching like dreeno addicts on a too-high glide.

His knees buckled, throwing him forward to the floor. Pain shot through his shoulder as he landed badly, tearing his tunic open. His backpack stymied him from rolling out of the kill zone. Two meters away, a loading bot rigged with a stunner shot him square in the chest.

Twilight descended. Light closed in on him as he lost control of everything. Stunners were especially effective on minders.

All he could do was watch as the shielder Fortezza smiled and danced his way through the flopping bodies, bending over each one. When got to Zade, he pulled the coat open and slapped a dormo patch on his neck. "Good dreams, *compagno*."

Zade kicked himself for jumping from one chaos storm into another. Twilight sucker-punched him into darkness.

2

He woke to blinding brightness. Turning his head away helped, but stiff neck muscles complained. His eyes felt gritty.

The rest of his body registered grievances. An aching left shoulder, sore spots on his back and butt, and an empty stomach demanded his attention. Not much he could do about them, since he appeared to be naked and strapped down on a high metal table. Flexible bands held his legs, torso, and arms tight.

His table was a couple of meters from a streaked, dull gray wall. Through the fading afterburn spots in his vision, he saw an untidy stack of dusty crates in the corner that made the room look more like a storeroom than a medical facility.

A piercing, shrill voice assaulted his ears. "Gossie! Tell the medics that 547 is finally awake."

Zade turned his head to the right. The long, narrow room held three more tables like his that turned out to be medical-style anti-gravity tables, otherwise known as corpse carts. They were all grounded and empty. A large, pale-skinned man holding a tablet and wearing a filthy hospital-yellow tunic stood in the doorway, yelling his conversation with someone inaudible outside the room.

"Tell 'em to punch their jets. The warden wants a personal ping after we test him." The man turned to look at Zade, then his tablet. "You're Lunaso, right?"

It took Zade two tries to get his throat working. "Yeah." Thirst moved to the top of his body's complaints. "Where am I?"

The man's face twisted with a half sneering, half sympathetic smile. "Nova Nine. Your new forever home."

Zade activated a bit of his talent. Pain lanced through his head, making his eyes water. It felt like he'd just come down from a ten-day glide on experimental chems. He powered through the pain, only to discover the black wall of a shielder. Releasing his talent eased the headache, but didn't banish it completely.

"Who is the warden?"

The pale-skinned man shook his head. "You'll know soon enough." He turned and exited.

Zade hadn't missed the fear that flashed across the pale man's face.

With nothing better to do, he inventoried his external body parts, relieved to discover they were all still there. Except his hair. From his reflection in the shiny trim around the floating light, he appeared to be completely bald. Not his favorite look, but he'd made worse fashion choices.

The contents of the room didn't tell him much more than he already knew, except the wall at the far end of the room looked like laser-sliced rock. Dust was everywhere. A ventilation system operated somewhere, because in the harsh overhead light, remnant swirls of dust still danced in a lazy downward spiral. Greens, reds, purples, and gold, like the colors that stained the pale man's tunic.

They landed on his skin, too. He firmly put aside thoughts of luxury cleansing spas, his favorite indulgence when he had funds and time off to spare. Freedom first; long, hot baths later.

The wall comp looked old, but the lights, including the floating orb above him, looked new. A square-shaped charred hole high up on one wall looked like it might once have held a clock display. It's where he'd have put one, at any rate.

Nova Nine could be a starship or space station, but dust shortened the lives of engines and enviro systems and would have been ruthlessly scrubbed and filtered. In his checkered career, he'd visited a few asteroid mines. They'd all had ubiquitous dust. Thank the universe that gravity generators and plates were built to be impervious to almost anything. Long-term zero-G was hard on human bodies.

His eyelids felt heavy, but he fought the temptation to drift off again. If he hoped to get out of his current predicament, he needed information, not sleep. He summoned up the tune of a rousing march to keep himself awake.

The only sounds in the room came from his heartbeats and breathing. Maybe his hearing protection implants were blocking other noises? If so, he hoped the medics had external diagnostics to check them. The implants worked by themselves. Better that than having a cybernetic controller installed and integrated with his brain.

He didn't like the ear implants, either, but he liked being deafened by starship engines even less. It was a pain in the ass to shuttle down to a civilized planet to visit the medical body shops for treatment. Only top-tier autodocs could fix natural hearing damage, and none of the outfits he'd worked for in the last twenty years had them. Traders couldn't afford the maintenance and supplies. Smugglers couldn't afford the space. Jackers didn't keep anything valuable, they sold it to the highest bidder. Like his last crew had planned to do with him.

The sound of multiple footsteps drew his attention to the doorway.

A woman and a man entered first, pulling a cart in with them. Their spotless medic tunics looked professional. The multiple instruments and scanners looked intimidating. He especially didn't like the large selection of chem jets, primed and ready to inject unknown chems into him.

A gaunt woman wearing a greenish-gray tunic and dusty brown pants slipped in through the doorway behind the medics but stayed just inside, leaning against the wall.

The big-shouldered woman with purplish skin tint and a loose halo of brilliant red and orange-streaked hair turned to look at the man with the cart. "Allergies?"

The man poked a tablet, making a holo display briefly. "Pharma tests say none."

"Good." She focused an assessing gaze on Zade's torso, then selected a jet from the rack and punched his left hip with it.

Stepping back, she crossed her arms and caught his gaze. "I'm Medic Peshek. Tell me your name."

They already had his name and quals, so it was hardly a secret. "Zade Lunaso." His hip felt numb. What was in that jet?

"He's telling the truth," said the gaunt woman near the door, with a bit of wheeze in her voice. Her accent was Standard English.

A sifter, then. He ordered himself to pay attention to his words.

"Ship specialty?" asked Peshek.

He shrugged one shoulder. "Whatever needs doing."

"Truth," said the sifter.

Peshek frowned. "Why were you out so long?"

"What day is it?" he asked. Now his whole left leg and part of his stomach felt numb.

Peshek glanced at the charred hole in the wall, then rolled her eyes in annoyance. She pulled back her sleeve to reveal a cuff-style percomp and made it display a large holo of the Galactic Standard Date and Time.

"The other three with you woke up thirty-six hours ago" She pointed a thumb toward the empty medical carts. Her tone seemed to accuse him of malingering.

Six days since he'd been lured and snared. Time he couldn't afford, considering he still had to figure out how to escape the current chaos cauldron he was in.

A familiar lassitude began to sneak into his thoughts. The sifter was trying to twiddle his brain receptors to make him more pliable and happy to babble out loud whatever crossed his mind. He smiled. The joke was on them. To hear his last ex-lover tell it, he had shit for brains. Can't get sense from shit.

Besides, now his whole left side was numb. His head sank downward, too heavy to keep tilted toward his visitors.

Peshek grimaced. "Shit!"

Zade smiled wider. "Exactly what she said!" It sounded garbled, but he knew what he meant.

Peshek grabbed another jet. "I thought you said no allergies!"

"All the tests were negative!" the tech protested.

Something shoved him sideways. A pounding heartbeat later, his veins caught fire. His implants couldn't block his own screams. Twilight, that back-alley thug, zeroed him again.

This time, he awoke to an impressive string of profanity that covered half a dozen of humanity's major languages.

The fire was gone. So was the numbness. A weird aftertaste made him wonder if they'd fed him hydroponic moss. Cautiously, he opened his eyes.

Same room. Peshek and her tech minion were still there, hovering watchfully. The tech now held a scanner that he was showing to Peshek.

She nodded, waving the scanner away. "That's better."

Peshek turned back to Zade. "What else are you allergic to besides sinamakri? Any other relaxers?"

"Most of them, actually. Pressors and vasopressors, too. Some endo-uptake inhibitors. Maybe a GABA energy-stim, but that might have been the contaminated Lautauro Spark I drank."

"Truth," said the sifter, who was now seated on the floor. She looked tired.

Peshek's mouth twisted in disdain as she poked at her tablet, then handed it to the tech. "When we're done here, find the pharma techs who ran the tests and space them."

"Yes, sir."

Zade couldn't tell from the tech's straight face if Peshek was joking or giving an actual order.

"Your turn, Bolerdi." Peshek motioned to the gaunt sifter. "I'd have to synthesize the right chems to make him pliant but not kill him, and that would take days." Peshek and the tech pulled the cart back and stepped out of the way.

Bolerdi stood and made a token attempt to brush the dust off her pants. She glanced at his naked body, but her expression didn't evince interest. "Low-level empath, huh?"

The languid feeling came sneaking back, meaning she was messing with his receptors again.

"That's what the CPS test said." He chose his words carefully. "I don't know low from high."

"Any other talents?" She looked distracted for a moment, then spat a curse. "You're telepath immune."

Interesting. Bolerdi was both a sifter and a telepath.

"So I'm told." That fact over-torqued the jets of most telepaths, and Bolerdi was no exception. Zade quite liked it in moments like this.

She listed the common minder talents — telepath,

sifter, healer, telekinetic, ramper, filer, fixer, forecaster — and made him specifically deny each one out loud.

Her expression hardened as she blew out a loud breath. "Activate your full empath talent now, or I'll tell them" — she tilted her head toward the medics — "to give you a cocktail that will make you beg for death."

Peshek selected a jet from the rack and gave him a pointed look.

Zade didn't see any option but to comply. The whole process was the brutal version of how the Citizen Protection Service tested every citizen in the Central Galactic Concordance when they turned twelve and again at age seventeen. He had experience with those.

Activating renewed his sharp headache and made his eyes water. Bolerdi contained her emotions well, but he still caught flavors of citrusy resentment mingled with bitter fear. Peshek felt like a porous wall, but the tech was a solid shielder, so he could be shielding Peshek, too.

"Can you make me feel happy? Or sad?" demanded Bolerdi.

"Not my skill set." He couldn't hold his talent any longer and let it go. The headache stayed, like he'd overexerted and was paying for it in blowback. Migraines tanked.

The unexpected wave of contentment that washed through him had to be her doing. He focused on the fact that he was being interrogated in a filthy room while strapped bare-ass naked to a corpse cart.

Her eyes narrowed. "Partial lie."

Frustration burned away the rest of the false contentment. "I can't manipulate emotions."

The headache made Zade's tone sharper than he'd intended. He tried to find his own calm. Instinct said if he didn't cooperate now, the consequences could be fatal.

Her expression turned sour. "Truth." She scratched her ear. "What's your bandwidth? How many people can you handle at once? Ten? A hundred? A thousand?"

The pointless question annoyed him. "I never counted."

"Did anyone train you to use your talent? CPS? Private?"

That was easy. "No."

"Truth." She stared at him for several long moments, then shook her head and turned to the medics. "The drug reaction fucked him up, so I can't push him any harder right now. But I'm not sensing anything but low empath. Your call."

Peshek put the jet back in the rack. "Let's not keep the warden waiting. He can have his recruiters test him again if he wants more assurance. I'll tell 'em we'll be in Processing."

ZADE SQUEEZED his eyes shut during the trip through the hallways. Dizziness warred with nausea if he watched the patterned ceiling, and the migraine pain was worse when he turned his head to the side.

Their destination turned out to be a large, square room with a high ceiling covered in light panels. They grounded the cart and got him to stand up.

It looked vaguely like a military ship's briefing room,

with a dozen benches in rows facing a low platform and a hazy display wall opposite the doorway. Dusty crates lined the back wall, filled with what turned out to be premade gray tunics and brown pants in various sizes, plus underwear, socks, and ankle-high stretch booties with thin soles.

Two people made him stand on a tailor's scanner, then dug in the crates to sort out gray and brown clothing for him. They worked hurriedly. He hugged the pants and tunic to his chest, pretending the bundle was soft and warm.

Bolerdi, who'd been lying on one of the benches, suddenly scrambled to her feet. She turned to face the doorway as she straightened her tunic.

Moments later, the warden arrived.

At least, Zade assumed the figure in the eye-popping red full-body purity cloak and distortion veil was the warden. The flowing, floor-length cloak hid everything but the width of his shoulders and a slight limp.

The two clothing suppliers backed up to the far wall, looking very much like they hoped not to be noticed. Peshek and her tech stood stiffly next to the grav cart with watchful attention. Bolerdi's wooden expression gave nothing away, but her eyes tracked the warden's movements.

Five people entered next. They wore matching contoured gold tunics, black pants, and high boots. One stood just behind the red-cloaked figure. The rest fanned out into the room, ending up near each of the occupants. Enforcers, Zade guessed. They all had skull jacks, and the one closest to the warden also wore a thick and intricate-looking tech collar.

Two more tall people parked themselves just outside the door, facing away. Their red flexin and shell-armored mech suits matched the warden's red cloak. They stood without moving. Something about them gave Zade a chill.

"You may call me Warden Kanogan." Standard English, and a man's baritone voice. Natural, rather than sound-processed, Zade thought. "I'm looking for new talents to join my team. You look a lot like a former employee of mine." Kanogan took a step forward. "He was a very dangerous man. Are you dangerous?"

After a long moment, Zade realized it wasn't just a rhetorical question. "Erm, no, sir."

The sophisticated distortion veil's constantly shifting shadows hid all but the vague shape of Kanogan's face. He turned toward Bolerdi. "Well?"

"Truth." She hesitated, then added, "He's telepath immune."

"Interesting." One of Kanogan's shoulders twitched as he turned back to Zade. "Turn around slowly." His confident tone suggested he was used to being obeyed. "Raise your arms. Let me see all of you."

Zade turned a slow full circle, wishing he was wearing the clothes instead of carrying them in one hand. Decades of ship living made him indifferent to his own nudity or anyone else's, but this was meant to make him feel vulnerable. It worked.

Kanogan shook his head. "As much as I'd love to chat, I'm on a tight schedule today."

Without warning, Kanogan raised a slender tube and punched Zade in the chest.

Agony took over as he collapsed. His limbs each tried to run in a different direction to get away from the pain. No shockstick ever felt like that.

When he finally stopped twisting like a tree snake, he realized he'd peed himself and his new clothes.

Kanogan lifted his hem and stepped back from the small yellow puddle. "Medic. Show me the front of his neck." One of Kanogan's boots had metal struts, suggesting he wore a partial exoframe under the cloak.

Peshek crouched next to Zade and pushed Zade's chin up and back, then shined a hand light. Now all Zade could see was Bolerdi's dusty ankle boots and the equally dusty calf-height black military boots of the enforcer who stood near her. After a long moment, Peshek released him and went back to her place near the cart.

Zade stayed still on the floor. He had no doubt anyone in the room would kill him instantly if the warden ordered it.

"He's of no use to me. Send him to the general population." Kanogan turned and headed through the door, followed by his silent entourage.

The others in the room stayed where they were until Bolerdi collapsed onto a bench, relief etched on her face.

Peshek and her technician used scanners on Zade, then helped him stand. "We'll clean you up before we turn you over to orientation."

In his youth, back when he'd lived on a planet, he'd once watched a winter eagle swoop down for a kill in the middle of a flock of wild geese huddled on a frozen lake.

The eagle stayed and leisurely ate its midday meal of goose. The others on the ice slowly sidled away, averting their gaze, pretending they hadn't seen anything. Peshek, Bolerdi, and the others all had that same look.

Zade made himself look on the positive side. At least he wasn't someone's lunch.

3

Julke had a bad feeling about the seam of ore that she and the other two prisoners were assigned to excavate. She'd learned to listen to her instincts, honed by nearly five hundred days of captivity in the asteroid mine that wasn't on anyone's star charts. Instinct, however, wasn't something she could believably explain to anyone else. She'd given up trying.

The working area was like many others. The unmanned mining bots created and stabilized gravity-plated tunnels to follow the meandering deposit of the target ore. In this seam, chofirium, a friable rock that looked like a sponge. But because drilling chofi created thick, billowing clouds of choking reddish purple dust, it took humans with hot rock cutters to do the actual extraction. The work area had to be water-saturated like a steam room, or even the cutter would clog.

Maybe her uneasiness had to do with the injured griffin she'd smuggled in with her. The little thing now rested in a nest of rags under a broken lens cover to keep the dust away. The hopper's engine housing kept it warm. She'd glued a tiny cast to the broken wing to give it time to heal. The griffin, which she'd named Moonlet, seemed more antsy than yesterday.

She neatened up the nest around the domestic kitten-sized body and tucked in its long, tufted tail under the cover. In the civilized galaxy, griffins were a venerable and perennially popular pet-trade species, designed to look like miniature griffins from pre-Flight mythology. The dozens of officially registered breeds all had bird heads, lion bodies, and wings, but the variations were endless. All the ones in Nova Nine were bird-light, with flat, downy feathers designed to mimic the look of fur. Little Moonlet had a gray, moon-shaped cloud pattern on its side. This breed of griffin charmed her with their tufted ears, bold topknots of springy feathers, and large, brilliant gold eyes.

Julke tried to project soothing care. She'd been told the griffins were like empaths, sensitive to human emotions. She believed it.

The guards regarded the feral populations of griffins as pests to be killed whenever possible. Prisoners who learned to respect and care for the lively, sneaky, and occasionally hilarious griffins knew better. Miraculously, four breeds of griffins had not only survived, but thrived in an unpredictable and dangerous asteroid. Humans who paid attention when griffins alerted to trouble tended to live longer.

She checked the hopper and adjusted the intake tube. Purple-red dust billowed out, then got sucked back into the collector bin. Only one more hour to go on their shift.

Professional   mine   operations   had   specially

engineered protective gear for human workers. Nova Nine issued deep-space exosuits intended for spacewalks. The mine's supply buyer seemed to have cornered the market on antique suits, regardless of design, then grafted on modern tactile gloves and oxygen concentrators with atmosphere readouts. The suits kept the dust out of the prisoners' lungs and grit off their skin. As a bonus, the built-in plumbing also enabled the mine operators to keep the prisoners working for a full twelve-hour shift, rather than having to allow bathroom or water breaks.

Some prisoners hated the invasive tubes and pads, not to mention drinking recycled water. To Julke, who'd grown up in the Volksstam city ships, exosuits were a fact of life.

She'd give anything to be back in the arms of her people. The information she'd uncovered was vital to their survival, and they didn't even know she had it. But each day in the mine drained her reservoir of hope of escape or rescue a little more. As it was, she was one of the longest-surviving prisoners. The work was risky and the environment unforgiving. Moreover, those were easy-glide rides compared to the warden's twisted whims and the live-subject experiments conducted by his pharma company partner.

And whirlpools of despair weren't improving her personal chances of survival, either. She ruthlessly jettisoned that spiral of thought and focused on the here and now.

She fished the fat cockroach corpse out of her suit's outer chest pocket and fed it to the recuperating griffin.

They'd eat almost anything, but she figured the concentrated protein would help the healing process.

Lantham, a tall man who'd been forcibly recruited, was operating the cutter. "Seam is angling up and toward left-axis again." The built-in communications system in her exosuit made it sound like he was standing right next to her instead of several meters away in a room full of noisy machinery.

He'd been an indie trader before being caught about a hundred days ago, and was a filer, with a minder talent for remembering everything he ever heard, saw, or experienced. Julke knew from personal experience that it was a two-edged forceblade. Some memories she'd trade anything to forget.

Sutrio, a mid-height woman who'd been caught by a similar trap, sat in the cab of the rolling jig that collected and separated the chofi from the worthless rock. "Spiral seams are bad."

She'd been a prisoner almost as long as Julke, but lately wasn't doing well. Sooner or later, the mine got to everyone. On her good days, she was an animal affinity, with the ability to exchange thoughts and emotions with animals. Thanks to her, most of the prisoners knew how to care for griffins, even the orphaned and injured.

Sutrio's full jig trundled slowly away from Lantham and to the hopper.

That left Julke to load the valuable chofi ore into the hopper, keep the waste out of everyone's way, and monitor the finicky enviro unit that generated air and humidity in the sealed work area. She could handle the extraction machines, but like most of the Volksstam, she was shorter and smaller than the two indie traders.

Her fourth job was to operate the scanner. "Lantham, move so I can update the materials map."

Lantham swung the cutter to the side and stepped back.

Julke pulled the scanner out of its pack and lugged it to where Lantham stood. She set it down, aimed it, and waited until it beeped the completion sequence. Like most of the mine's equipment, it was old and spent a lot of time with the repair techs. It was supposed to send the data to the mine's hypercube immediately, but sometimes the techs had to do it manually once it got back to the habitable area. The central AI analyzed the twisting seam's adjacent morphology and, if needed, directed the tunneling machines to install a new set of gravity plates and light pillars during their sleep shift.

On her way back with the scanner, she checked the temporary airlock again to make sure the inner seal was tight against the tunnel walls. As she did, she saw through the transparent doorway that neither mech-suited guard was stationed outside like they should have been.

Julke waved to get Sutrio's attention, then pointed toward the temporary airlock, made the sign for guards, then the signs that meant they weren't there.

Their absence was good and bad. Good, because some guards were assholes who made the shift miserable. Dajoya was the worst, but she had competition. Bad in case of trouble with the equipment or with the valuable but volatile materials they were extracting. And prisoners couldn't get back to the cells without an escort.

The guards were spread too thin. Especially after the big blowout about sixty days before that had killed twenty prisoners and nine guards.

She'd heard the mine was upping the pay and benefits to attract more candidates. The job would be a tough sell. Guards had to have mining experience, be minder shielders, and agree to stay one standard galactic year. And according to believable rumors, candidates also had to agree to let a minder cleaner erase key memories so they couldn't betray the existence of the rogue asteroid.

They'd just completed two more jig loads when they were interrupted by an announcement from Security Operations Control.

"Workgroup 17-C. Pause operations and stand by for inspection. Acknowledge and report individually." She pegged the mid-range voice as belonging to the regular Admin tech for their shift, rather than one of the security staff or equipment techs.

"Acknowledged," responded Lantham. "Cycling rock cutter's power off." He hit the switch, then laid the heavy cutter aside, careful to avoid the hot wand that could burn a foot off in a nanosecond.

Sutrio set the jig to idle and announced her action. The mine had long ago given up using visual feeds to monitor prisoners. No camera survived more than a few hours in an active excavation area.

Julke turned the humidifier down, then hurried over to the hopper. She scooped up the griffin and its nest and looked for a place to hide them.

Sutrio climbed out of the jig's cab, then opened the built-in tool box on the side and pointed. Julke tried to send soothing apologies to the griffin for the rough handling as she crammed the nest into the tight space. Sutrio closed the door, then stood in front of it.

Julke ran to the hopper and powered it down. "Hopper offline."

The comms systems in their suits let everyone talk to each other without shouting. But it also let the guards and staff overhear every word of every conversation. Prisoners had developed sign language for conveying private information.

Lantham gave the sign for *what the hell?*

It had been a while since the last inspection, maybe before Lantham arrived. Inspections usually meant equipment was missing. Julke gave the signs for *probably nothing* and *trim your jets.*

Moments later, the airlock doorway opened. Two guards stepped in, each wearing the light and flexible state-of-the-art mech suits that all the tunnel guards had.

Lhap Cho and Dajoya were escorting a prisoner she didn't recognize. Or more accurately, an exosuit suit she didn't recognize and a face she couldn't see.

Lhap Cho stepped aside and pointed toward the prisoner. "This is Lunaso 3006. He went through full orientation a couple of hours ago. We added him to your workgroup's comms net." The guard's accent spoke of a Mandarin heritage.

Lhap Cho pointed to Julke. "Defayensdytr 1351 is your trainer." He turned to give her a pointed look. "He's all yours."

Julke nodded once, hiding her dismay. The last thing she needed was to be stuck with a *beschaafd* noob from the

Concordance's part of the galaxy, and be held responsible for his actions. At best, their workgroup would take a quota hit and be forced to work extra to make up for it. At worst, he'd be a bumbling *klojo* who'd get her punished or get them all killed.

The other guard, Dajoya, stepped forward. "Line up for inspection."

Lhap Cho shook his head. "We don't have time–"

Dajoya overrode him with forceful volume. "Yes, we do. Shitting griffins got into the staff food storeroom again. Warden wants them eradicated."

Lhap Cho waved an arm dismissively. "Have at it, then." He didn't bother to hide his exasperation.

Julke waved to the noob. "Lunaso. Come stand next to me." She edged left to give him room.

He glanced briefly at the guards, then walked to where she pointed to her right. He was taller than she'd thought, and wide-shouldered. At least he seemed comfortable moving in an exosuit.

Lantham and Sutrio moved to stand next to the noob.

Dajoya climbed up to look inside the hopper control cab and poke around in the tool compartment. She jumped down, generating a cloud of dust as her heavy gravity boots landed.

Her expression became more irritable as she waved the dust away and glared at Julke. "You, pirate-clan puke. Turn up the mister."

Julke blanked her expression as she crossed to the enviro unit and did as ordered. If they ran out of water before the end of the shift, Dajoya and Lhap Cho would be the ones bringing them another tank.

Dajoya climbed up and into the jig's cab, then leaned out to try the handle of the jig's toolbox. "Why won't this open?"

Julke's heart sank. The little griffin Moonlet had nowhere to hide if Dajoya got the door open.

Sutrio clasped her hands behind her back. "It's jammed."

Dajoya jumped down and pulled out one of her favorite energy weapons, a high-res beamer. "Then I'll un-jam it."

"No!" The word was out before Julke could censor herself.

"Stop!" Lhap Cho lunged at Dajoya to clamp his gloved hand tightly onto her arm. "Why are you always shooting shit?"

Dajoya pulled herself away from his grip, but re-holstered her beamer. "Touch me again and I'll kill you."

The heated menace in her tone didn't seem to faze Lhap Cho. "Hit a pure chofi deposit with a beamer and you won't have to because we'll *all* be dead."

"Workgroup 17-C. Resume operations. Guards Lhap Cho and Dajoya, report to Security Operations Center immediately. Acknowledge and report." The tone brooked no argument.

Lhap Cho stalked away from Dajoya stiffly, his expression hard. When she turned his direction, he gave her the universal gesture for "fuck you."

Suddenly, the noob Lunaso stepped out of line, in front of Julke, facing the guards. "Am I supposed to stay here or come with you?"

Before Julke could react, he stiffened, then crumpled

to the ground, twitching. His fall revealed that Dajoya now held a stunner.

Dajoya bent over to sneer at Lunaso. "Don't speak unless you're spoken to. I'm betting you won't last a ten-day." She straightened, then pointed the stunner at Julke and pressed the trigger.

Familiar fire lit up Julke's body. Her knees collapsed, taking her down to lie twitching next to the enviro unit. Even after taking hundreds of stuns, it never got any easier to ride out the pain and disorientation.

"That's for insubordination, pirate filth. Even the five of you left is too many–" Dajoya's triumphant gloat was cut short by Lhap Cho forcefully pulling her away.

Through the brain fog caused by the stunner, she thought she heard Lhap Cho hissing at Dajoya as he forced her through the room's temporary doorway. "You will *not* cut into my bonus or get me killed when I only have twenty-eight more days in this hellhole!"

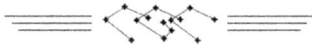

THIRTY MINUTES LATER, all of Julke's limbs belonged to her again. She'd spent the last ten minutes of conscious recovery time realizing that Lunaso had somehow known what Dajoya intended.

Like all guards, she was a shielder, but the hot-tempered woman was also a ramper who could draw a weapon faster than anyone else in the mine, even the warden's red-armored guardians. If Zade was a ramper, too, able to use his minder talent to improve his speed and strength, he still couldn't have blocked the shot in time, much less gotten a full question out.

That pointed to him being a sifter, able to detect impending violence. However, unless Dajoya had dropped her shield, he'd have to be high level to have felt it coming. If so, he'd have to be an expert at hiding the strength of his minder talent. Otherwise, he'd have been sent to the warden. Kanogan kept high-level talents for his own staff, willing or not. He had ugly ways of making them comply.

Since it took a minimum of three people to work the seam, Dajoya's impulsive act gave Lantham and Sutrio an unexpected rest period, too. Julke took satisfaction in knowing both guards likely got reamed for impacting mine productivity.

Julke caught Lantham's eye and tilted her head toward the temporary airlock. *Are the guards there?* she signed.

Yes, but different ones, he replied. He made the signs for two guards who usually worked in the prison block area. *They don't know the equipment. And Dajoya's second shot flatlined the scanner.*

Julke stood, testing her balance. The usual aching in her joints and ringing in her ears would soon pass. She wondered how many more stunner hits she could take before they did irreversible damage.

Sutrio and Lantham climbed to their feet. After a moment, Lunaso did, too. He got up gracefully — not easy in an exosuit — and his expression seemed alert and watchful. If he was hurting, he hid it well.

According to the clock display in her helmet, it was only twenty minutes to shift end.

Julke spoke out loud. "Are we on schedule or on overtime?"

"On schedule," said Lantham.

Thank the universe for small favors. They could have been forced to work extra hours immediately to make their daily quota.

She nodded. "That's enough time to show Lunaso what he needs to know."

They each took turns demonstrating the equipment, starting with the cutter and ending with the hopper.

Sutrio caught Julke's eye and pointed to the jig's tool box, then to the front seam of her own exosuit and made the sign for griffin.

Julke hesitated, not wanting to get her friend in trouble, but gave in and accepted the offered help. Sutrio's animal affinity talent made it much easier for her to keep the little injured creature quiet while she smuggled it back into the habitation area.

Drawing Lunaso toward the enviro unit, she told him to call her Julke so he wouldn't mangle her family name, then gave him a detailed briefing on the humidifier, oximeter, and dust particulate counter. She also pointed out the air quality meter that had been added to his exosuit's upper left arm and identified the separate displays for external and internal readings. The suit's heads-up display in their helmets, she told him, only showed the date and time, internal supplies levels, and whether or not the suit was sealed.

Because she was watching, she noticed that he noticed Sutrio was doing something at the jig. She also noticed he didn't ask. Grudgingly, and despite her initial instincts, she had to respect a man who knew how to keep his eyes and ears open and his mouth shut.

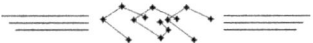

THE GUARDS OPENED the mine-side airlock and motioned Julke's workgroup and one other inside the decontamination transition zone. They'd had to wait while Julke handed over the scanner for repair, so they were the last group through for the shift change. The long, rectangular chamber could hold twenty in a pinch, but doing so created traffic jams. She motioned for Lunaso to hold on to one of the holdfasts, then pointed to a wall display showing a countdown.

"Air blasters run for one minute when that hits zero. The timer resets twice more, once for a thirty-second chem spray, once for water jets." She pointed to the air nozzles. "Keep your helmet away from these if you ever want to see through it again."

It has been too long since she'd had to train a new prisoner. "Hey, Lantham, what am I forgetting?"

"Suit scrub." Lantham pointed to Zade's hips. "After the chem spray, open your waste pockets so the pressurized water cleans them out. Otherwise, you'll have to do it by hand when you pull your pads."

Sutrio tilted her chin toward the airlock at the far end of the exit zone. "Suits come off in the locker room. Did they give you clothes?"

"Yes." Lunaso watched Lantham, then mimicked the man's feet-apart, bent-knee stance.

The display turned bright blue.

Julke braced herself. "Here it comes."

The decontamination procedure was like being in a live-experience simulation of a multi-scenario disaster. Dust rose into a maelstrom, then got sucked down through the grate beneath their gravity boots. Orange chem spray coated everything and dripped slowly. The second the flood waters came, she opened her suit's pockets and angled them toward the outlets. Most Nova Nine equipment was antique, but thank the gods of Chaos, the mine's sophisticated environmental systems were new and state-of-the-art. They'd recapture all the air, water, dust, and waste, then filter and recycle it.

She belatedly glanced at Zade to check that he was okay, but he seemed to have figured it out.

When the water stopped, the wider, heavier airlock at the other end of the tunnel irised open, revealing the habitation side's cavernous locker room. A hundred or more stationary hooks hung from the ceiling, about half holding clothes or exosuits. The mine had been steadily losing workers. Lunaso was the first noob mine worker they'd had in a quarter-year. Were there more?

She unsealed her helmet as she helped him find the numbered hook where he'd left his clothes. She stayed long enough to make sure he knew how to get out of an exosuit. The fact that he triggered all the releases and opened his helmet before pulling off his gloves made her think he'd logged a lot of hours in a suit.

"The orientation vid said I'm supposed to give my suit to a guard for inspection and recharge." His voice sounded as tired as he looked.

She shook her head. "Not enough staff to do that." She pointed to the hook with his clothes. "Pull the pads and just hang it. The guards will scan them later and bring them to the cells after dinner. Pads go in the blue bins along the walls for recycling. We'll get fresh pads, water, and an oxy charge in the morning before the shift starts." Pointing to the door to the hallway, she added, "Meet me there when you're dressed."

Weaving her way through a forest of clothes and ducking the people getting into them, she found her own clothes and changed quickly. Her exosuit had more patches than original material, but the internal systems were good. Still, she was glad to be out of it for a while. The constant pressure to precisely choose every single word she said made her shoulders tight as a drum.

She dropped off her pad, then was surprised to see Lantham and Sutrio waiting for her near the open door instead of queuing up for the walk to the dining hall. She let several prisoners go by her before stepping close to Sutrio. "Not hungry?"

Sutrio's eyes went a little jittery as she shook her head. "I'm eating for two."

Instant remorse lanced through Julke. She'd been so caught up in making sure Lunaso got along that she'd forgotten Sutrio was still carrying the injured griffin. "I'll take it."

"Her," corrected Sutrio. "She's fine with me. Just give me cover."

"What is she?" asked Lunaso.

Julke twitched, startled by Lunaso's quiet approach. She ordered herself to pay better attention.

Both Lantham and Sutrio looked away, leaving the decision to her.

Lunaso could be a spy. A wily spy would do something like ingratiate himself with the prisoners, such as taking a stunner shot meant for one of them. On the other hand, Dajoya was unholy chaos in a mech suit and couldn't play-act for shit. Plus, all the previous spies the warden had sent were exposed within hours. Nova Nine used minders as workers because they were easier to catch and no one important missed them. Spies were no match for a prison population full of mental talents.

Julke rarely activated hers. She'd convinced the warden's intake interrogators she was only a filer with a smidgeon of empathy. Using any other talent might prompt any nearby sifters to deliver her to the warden's elite interrogation team for a more thorough evaluation. She'd give them a fight, but had no doubt they'd eventually pry her brain open like a griffin's eggshell.

But right now, she was the best person around to get a calibration on Lunaso. She fought the after-effects of the stun shot to cautiously activate her empathy talent. Lantham was sad and depressed as usual, and Sutrio was like a miscalibrated flux drive engine with emotions spiking randomly. Lunaso was bewildered, scared, and lonely. And an empath.

His talent rose to meet hers. For a brief moment, the entrancing warmth of his essence danced with hers. His gold-brown eyes seemed to draw her in.

Alarmed, she slammed a lock on her talent and made herself step back, clearing her throat. He might be a danger to her, but very likely not a spy. "In answer to your question, she's a griffin."

His eyes widened. "The miniature-lion-with-wings kind? When Lhap Cho and Dajoya took me to meet you, she shot at one with her beamer."

"In the tunnels?" Lantham swore a vicious oath. "She's a blowout waiting to happen."

Lunaso edged closer. "Can I help?"

Julke instinctively wanted to trust him. But then again, trusting a man had landed her in Nova Nine. Still, building mutual trust with all the other prisoners — and griffins — had kept her alive so far.

She caught Sutrio's eye and spoke quietly. "They'll have put Lunaso in our cell cluster. If you both skip dinner, I'll smuggle food for two." She tilted her chin toward Sutrio's middle. "Two and a half."

Lunaso cleared his throat. "Call me Zade. I was raised in a group home. I have, er, smuggling experience." His fingers waved in a quick, subtle fan.

Julke had heard that the five hundred member planets of the Central Galactic Concordance had a lot of homes like those. Her people used them to frighten wayward children into behaving.

She looked to Sutrio. "You good?"

"Yes." Her friend's eyes jittered. "Bring me dense protein. Seaweed-rice. Chocolate."

Julke hoped Sutrio was communing with the hidden griffin and not about to go off the rails, as had been happening to her more often lately. "Deal."

Lantham nudged Sutrio's elbow with his. "Want company?"

"No, go eat." A smile ghosted across her face. "You can be their lookout."

At the guard station, Sutrio split off to join the small group being escorted to the cells. Julke, Lantham, and Zade were the last to join the much larger group headed for the dining hall.

Prisoners weren't supposed to talk during transfers, but most guards ignored quiet conversations. Since they weren't being monitored, Julke took the opportunity to tell Zade a few truths that weren't in the prisoner orientation vids.

"The tunnels are a chaotic labyrinth. Don't go in them without safety equipment, and don't ever go alone. Getting lost is the number two killer of noobs. Our exosuits don't have maps like the guards' mech suits do. The Security Operations Center only activates a suit's trace-tracker if they know you're missing, and they're only good for about thirty meters. You'll die of thirst before anyone ever finds you."

Zade nodded and scratched the back of his smooth head.

She spoke fast. "We can talk here, but watch what you say when your exosuit helmet is sealed. All comms are actively monitored by AI and humans. So are processing facility workstations. The guards will stun you if you speak in anything besides Standard English while on official comms, especially if the warden is around."

"No problem," said Zade. "That's my primary language. But why do stunners work when we're wearing exosuits?"

Julke moved closer. "The maintenance lab deliberately

fries the static countervailers in them. Supposed to be a secret."

Lantham lowered his head and spoke softly. "Lots of things will get you stunned. Disobeying orders from guards or staff, or arguing with them. Like today with you and Julke."

"Same goes with pharma techs." added Julke. At Zade's puzzled expression, she added, "I'll tell you about them later."

Lantham ticked off items with his fingers. "Fighting with another prisoner. Minor assault, minor theft." He made a rude hissing sound. "Or with assholes like Dajoya, just breathing."

Julke nodded. They were getting close to the dining hall, and there was still so much he needed to know to survive. "Some things get you seriously hurt and stuffed in an autodoc while you heal. Don't ever touch a guard without permission, not even in self-defense. They'll shoot you on sight if they catch you unescorted in the forbidden areas. Making quota is job number one, so don't damage a prisoner enough that they can't work. No equipment sabotage, either."

"Yeah," said Lantham. "Endangering lives gets you disabled in a nanosecond. If it was deliberate, the prisoners would probably hold you for the guards."

"What about escape attempts?" asked Zade.

Lantham sighed. "You seem like a pleasant person, so I'd hate to see you suffer. Don't try it. They'll hurt you, kill you, or worse."

Zade's expression seemed earnest, but she thought she saw a brief pattern of 'challenge accepted' in his emotional aura. Which her own talent shouldn't be detecting in the first place. Damnit. That stunner shot must have left her more out of control than she thought.

"Look," she said, "everyone dreams of freedom. Noobs like you, especially. But no one has ever succeeded, and the warden gets twisted thrills from making gory public examples of failures." The line slowed as the people in front began filing through the dining hall entrance scanners. "Nova Nine is a dark relic from your notorious Central League era, and its elements are worth mega-trillions. He'd kill every one of us to keep its secrets."

4

In the ten days since Zade's arrival, Julke had felt a renewed sense of precious time slipping by. Maybe because her bad feeling about the vein they'd been working hadn't gone away. Or maybe because she was seeing everything new again while teaching him how to stay alive.

She hung her clothes on the locker room hook, then finished stretching and twisting in her exosuit to get it situated on her body. Thankfully, she no longer had to smuggle an injured griffin. Moonlet was already flying short distances again, even though the wing splint only came off yesterday.

The locker room was beginning to stink again. She sealed her helmet early, or she'd be smelling it for the whole work shift. When the odors got obnoxious enough, facility maintenance would seal the room and give it a chem bath. Then it would smell like caustic insecticide and fungicide for a week.

She glanced around for Zade and found him with Lantham, already waiting at the airlock, helmet sealed.

He'd turned out to be an amazingly quick study, which he'd attributed to his variety of starship jobs across the galaxy. Based on his experience, she suspected Zade was older than the mid-forties he looked. And his lively interest in everything might be part of it. He soaked up knowledge like a sponge. At mealtimes, he cajoled even the surliest of prisoners into conversations.

She also found him unexpectedly easy to talk to, which should have been tripping her warning bells but wasn't. She'd like to blame it on the unexpected mesh of their empathic talents. However, she knew she had a weakness for people who were sexy, noble, and kind. He ducked confrontation unless he was defending other prisoners. The only thing against him so far was his habit of humming or whistling tunes in quiet moments.

And the griffins adored him. She'd seen an increasing number clinging to his cell wall to sleep in his cell at night. If he got up in the dark, at least three sets of fire-bright eyes would be watching him. Though it was possible they were hoping for the treats he'd been successfully smuggling from the dining hall, she'd only ever seen Sutrio's cell with that many griffins.

Even downhearted Lantham, who missed his family deeply, seemed less gloomy when Zade worked the extraction equipment with him. They shared a love of vintage starships and a dreamer's desire to collect them.

To top it off, he was nova hot. Not that she'd deliberately looked, but she couldn't help noticing when they all stripped twice a day to get in and out of exosuits. Wide-shouldered, wide and well-muscled rib cage, and undeniably stellar ass and thighs. The dark stubble of hair on his head hinted at a jacker-style mohawk if it grew back. Beautiful brown skin, unmarred by scars, though mine work would change that.

Unsurprising for someone from the Central Galactic Concordance, where healthcare and anti-aging maintenance was a foundation right for all citizens. Hell, Lantham looked early fifties but had been celebrating his one hundred and nineteenth birthday the day of his capture.

While operating in CGC territory, she'd taken advantage of a medical and cosmetic body shop or two herself. Volksstam traditionalists sneered, but she didn't care. Her public position had been that of a private trade broker at the outer edge of CGC territory. Altering her appearance and dressing the part kept the CGC military from singling her out as the hated pirate clan. Her indie trader and frontier planet government contacts knew she had access to unique Volksstam goods and services and didn't ask questions.

Julke turned, expecting to see Sutrio getting into her suit. Instead, the woman was naked and kneeling, violently expelling her breakfast onto the floor. The other prisoners were giving her a wide berth.

Julke quickly unsealed her helmet and dropped to one knee. She swallowed hard against the stomach-turning stench that threatened to choke her. "Do you need a medic?"

Sutrio shook her head, then wiped her mouth with her forearm. "What I need is my brain-chem balancers. Fucking pharma researchers deactivated my implants because they were invalidating their fucking drug trials." Her stomach heaved again and she coughed.

That explained Sutrio's increasingly odd behavior. Julke kicked herself for not asking her friend about it sooner. "What do you want me to do?"

"Go with Lantham and Zade. I'll stay here and tell the guards I'm supposed to ask to see Medic Peshek." The corner of Sutrio's mouth twitched. "She hates the pharma assholes almost as much as we do."

Julke caught Sutrio's eye. "I'm sorry I didn't notice you were in trouble."

Sutrio sat back on her heels. "I didn't tell you. Nothing you could've done about it." Her head tilted toward the airlock. "Enjoy the party without me."

Julke hesitated, then reluctantly stood and made her way to the airlock, sealing her helmet on the way. She spoke out loud so the Admin tech for their shift would hear. "Sutrio is sick." She made the sign for pharma, though only Lantham would understand it.

Clever though he was, Zade only knew the basics of the prisoner's sign language. And he'd have to find out for himself what a chaos-bender it was to be in a pharma test group.

As she'd expected, Admin issued orders a few moments later. "*Workgroup 17-C. Proceed to the assigned area. You have enough workers to complete this shift.*"

Their assigned guards, Lhap Cho and Etellia, escorted them into the working area and gave Julke a pack with a new materials scanner. They sealed the airlock, then took their usual place outside it.

Julke showed Zade how to juggle hopper operation

and enviro monitoring duties. When she passed Lantham as he stood next to the jig, she used sign language to tell him that on the way in, she'd seen seven griffins in the tunnels heading in the opposite direction.

Lantham frowned, then looked toward the airlock. "We forgot to tell Zade about the emergency exit procedure."

It was cold comfort that Lantham also recognized the griffin exodus as a bad omen.

Zade paused on the first rung of the hopper's side ladder. "The orientation vid said to stay in the work area if there's trouble."

Julke made a rude gesture in prisoner sign language. "The vid is old. If the extraction process accidentally mixes enough chofirium, rhybarium, and xeronium together, there's a good chance it'll react sooner or later. You'll feel a vibration like a decompensating flux engine. If you do, or someone yells 'blowout,' run like a meteor is on your tail through the blue-striped extraction tunnels to the surface refinery. The guards will be running. too. Follow them if you can. Their suits have lights and current maps so they don't get lost in the labyrinth. They don't want to become one with the universe before their time, either."

Lantham frowned. "Don't get the bright idea to hitch a ride on an ore cart. It'll kill you."

Zade started to speak, then made a face. "Got it." His expression looked frustrated, like he wanted to ask a dozen questions.

Julke sympathized, but better explanations would have to wait until they weren't being monitored.

She picked up the cutter and powered it up. It was going to be a long shift.

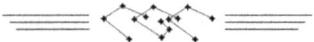

A MUCH-IMPROVED SUTRIO arrived several hours later to take over the cutter. Julke relieved Zade of the duty to move the trash tailings out of their way and keep the airlock entryway clear.

Sutrio unexpectedly set the cutter down. When Julke went to see if Sutrio was in trouble again, her friend pointed to the lower left corner of the gravity plate. "Look."

She didn't know what she was supposed to see until she caught the unmistakable thrash of a griffin tail. Unlike the common griffins like Moonlet, the stealth breed of griffins shunned the busier human habitation areas. Only Sutrio's animal-affinity talent would have noticed it.

Stealth griffins looked as flat as a solar cell. Their feathers were dusty mottled gray, and could color-morph to blend into the rocky scenery. This one was lying flat up against the wall where the plate was embedded. It must have gotten in during the downtime and been there all morning.

With a glance toward the airlock doors, Julke spoke for the benefit of the guards. "I'll get the scanner."

As she went back to get it, she made the sign for griffin so the others would know what was happening.

She needn't have worried about Zade remembering what that sign meant. He idled the hopper, then jumped down. "I'll shadow you."

"Good idea. It's a newer model." Julke pulled the unit out of its pack and led him to the right spot and pointed.

In case the guards were looking, she made a show of setting up the scanner and setting it to run. Zade hunkered down next to her, but all his attention was on the animal.

The griffin stood and shook itself. Without warning, it sprang up and landed on the shoulder of Zade's suit, then wrapped its thick, barbed tail around the back of his helmet. Within moments, the griffin's feathers mimicked the colors of Zade's suit.

A wondrous smile lit up his face. "Hello, little one."

Julke cleared her throat loudly. "Yes, that's right, the *little* readout is the *one* to watch."

He turned to her, wide-eyed, and made the sign for "sorry."

She waved away his apology. Everyone should have an enchanted moment like that now and again.

Sutrio laughed silently and held out her gloved hand to the griffin. It opened its beak and worked its throat like it was vocalizing. Luckily, the machinery noise covered it, he guards might investigate, otherwise.

The griffin pecked at Zade's helmet and vocalized again.

Sutrio's eyes jittered a moment. Her expression went slack.

The griffin launched from Zade's shoulder and flew toward the airlock. It veered away at the last moment and circled back around toward Zade.

"Blowout!" Sutrio's voice was loud and sharp.

Julke's stomach went leaden as she scrambled to her feet, stumbling to avoid the still-cycling scanner.

Sutrio slowed only to pull the cutter's emergency cutoff, then bolted toward the airlock.

Julke grabbed Zade's shoulder and pointed to the airlock where Sutrio was headed. "Run!"

The man rose fast and lunged forward, only pausing to help Lantham get off the jig's ladder. Astonishingly, the stealth griffin latched itself onto Zade's shoulder again as he ran.

At the airlock, Sutrio punched the emergency exit controls. Both doors irised open. "Blowout!" she yelled again as she charged into the tunnel.

By the time Julke passed the door, the guards were already ahead of Sutrio. The bright lights on their mech suits made them easy to track.

The angled blue stripes of the extraction tunnel made her dizzy, especially when the tunnel randomly changed direction and orientation. Down suddenly became sideways, but she had to keep running. Focusing on the gravity-plated floor helped, but her stomach was not on board with the effort. With her short legs, she had to take more steps than the others just to keep up.

Her heavy breathing created brief fog clouds on her helmet until the suit's systems recaptured the moisture. Only the daily physical work she did in the mine kept her in any condition at all, but she could already feel her knees creaking.

Still, the rhythmic pumping of her arms and legs reminded her of her childhood. She'd run down her *familieschip*'s longest corridors, hair loose and whipping behind her like a solar sail, arms stretched back like a slant-wing shuttle. Imagining she could take flight and go wherever in the galaxy the bright, beckoning stars led her.

Incongruously, she heard chanting. It took her a couple dozen steps to realize Zade was singing something as he ran, puffing out the tune between breaths and footfalls. It'd been too long since she'd heard actual music. He had a soothing singing voice. Maybe he'd sing the entire song sometime so she could call up the memory whenever she wanted.

After running for what seemed like kilometers, the tunnel's stripes abruptly ended and the corridor color became all bright yellow. Hope shot through her. They'd made it to the refinery before the danger the little griffin had warned them about.

After she ran through the shuttle-sized door, one of their guards punched the controls. The heavy incalloy blast doors closed behind her.

Slowing to a standstill, throat dry as her chest heaved, she was relieved to discover the refinery floor had at least fifty heavily-breathing prisoners, nearly half the current population. Their presence killed her insidious worry that Sutrio had called a false alarm. The punishment would have been harsh if she had.

Zade was bent at the waist, hands on his flexed knees, gasping for air. Sutrio and Lantham were nearby, with her helping Lantham to stay upright as his breath bellowed, fogging his helmet.

Julke waved to get their attention, then motioned for them to follow. She led their little group to an area out of the traffic pattern and with some privacy. Once all the doors were sealed and the guards got organized, they'd order the prisoners to sit along the walls. Picking a good spot now meant that once they were allowed to open their helmets and unseal their suits, they wouldn't also have to smell the chemical stink from the refinery circulation vents.

Besides, Zade needed the shadows. Otherwise, anyone looking at him for long might notice his suit had an asymmetrical, griffin-shaped lump on one shoulder.

After the other three were situated, she allowed herself to sit, back the rock wall, and drop her head between her knees. All the muscles and joint in her body were already stiffening up, her ankle tendons especially. The medics wouldn't waste precious autodoc meds on routine body maintenance for prisoners.

She tried to be grateful that gods of Chaos had let her survive another brush with death, but she was still furious with them for sending her to Nova Nine in the first place.

5

NOVA NINE FACILITY • GDAT 3243.117

Z ade stood and stretched, then took a couple of sidesteps to look at the clock display embedded in the refinery's rough-hewn wall. It claimed they'd been there for four hours. Based on how numb his butt was from sitting on the hard, cold, gravity-plated floor, it felt twice as long.

Almost the second after he'd sat on the floor next to Julke, the griffin on his shoulder had climbed up the wall behind him and into the shadows. By the time the guards came around to record his prisoner ID and tell him he could open his helmet and remove his gloves, but not take the suit off, meeting the little griffin seemed like an isolation delusion.

According to Julke, they'd get an idea of how big the blowout was based on how long they were stuck in the refinery. If they were all still there after eight hours, the news would be bad. The last blowout had killed more than thirty prisoners and guards. And lucky him, he'd been in the first group of replacements.

One good thing about the exosuits was that comms powered off when helmets were open. At least they wouldn't have to watch what they said. The guards had already stepped out of their mech suits, leaving the empty units standing in a huddle like they were discussing where to go for shore leave. The refinery workers on the levels above all wore open exosuits, but they also wore ankle shackles that kept them at their stations.

Thoughts kept tumbling in his head like cargo that hadn't been tied down before atmosphere liftoff. After recovering from the thrill-ride of a run, he'd failed at napping like Lantham and Sutrio. Julke looked dozy, with a half-lidded gaze fixed on her boots, but her dexterous fingers twitched like they wished they were braiding something.

Brushing off his backside out of habit, he sat back down and stretched his legs out straight. He turned his ankle to tap Julke's boot with his. "If you're staying awake because you're responsible for me, I promise to behave." *Or at least not get caught.*

She shook her head. "Can't sleep." She circled a finger to encompass the room. "Too many uncontained."

Now that he thought about it, he realized the only crowds in the mine were at mealtime. The cell layout kept all the prisoners in small groups surrounded by thick walls. His usual working environment on starships commonly put meters of incalloy between him and the rest of the crew. He wasn't used to having to keep his empath talent tamped down for long periods. No wonder he couldn't nap.

And if he was ruthlessly frank with himself, spending

idle time so close to Julke made him want to activate his talent rather than contain it.

She intrigued him. Her attractive, strong-angled features and muscled small body belied his mistaken first impression that she was delicate. And her pale skin and emerald-colored, intricately braided hair complimented her mesmerizing blue eyes.

As much as he liked the shape of her, though, the one brush with her empath talent had left an indelible imprint on him. Maybe it was her pirate clan…, no, Volksstam heritage, but he'd never felt such a strong sense of compatibility. Like reuniting with a close friend he'd somehow forgotten. Even now, she riveted his attention when he should be focusing on escape plans.

Deliberately looking away, he eyed the refinery equipment to see what he could identify. Not much, unfortunately. What he knew about raw materials processing would make for a very short conversation. Furthermore, before watching the orientation vids, he'd never heard of the three dangerous elements they were extracting and still had no clue why they were so valuable.

Of more immediate interest was a crowd of ore carts that occupied the far end of the space. He wondered how many more the mine had, and if they were used for anything else besides taking extracted ore from full hoppers and transporting it through the tunnels to the processing center. For example, could they go to the pressurized freight hangar or the exterior landing pad with refined ore to load for sale? Maybe they went to other useful places, too. With the right tools, he could disable defenses and fool monitoring tech, but not minders. But did the mine have enough guards to check each cart?

Leaning forward to touch his toes gave him the opportunity to eye the center area. The few mine guards who had ended up in the refinery had commandeered padded chairs and a couple of floating desks. They moved them to a spot that gave them a good view of the prisoners scattered about on the cavernous refinery floor. The guards barely glanced at the refinery workers who were chained to their stations, and didn't look at the ceiling at all.

"Sutrio said my stowaway stealth griffin went up to join the dracos." He kept his voice barely above a whisper. The guards had given up enforcing the "no talking" rule after the first thirty minutes, but no sense in being obvious about it. "What are those?"

"Another griffin species. Bigger, with broader wings. They nest in sponge rock and like heights. If you hear hissing, it's probably them." She flicked a glance upward. "I think the original miners found this closed void and decided it'd be a good place for the refinery. The sponge rock up top has thousands of nooks and crannies for griffin nests."

The chofi seam they'd been working had a lot of sponge rock, too. The orientation vids said it contained trapped oxygen that the refinery separated out to augment the enviro systems. On starships, they'd need a good supply of carbon dioxide for the hydroponics systems. Did sponge rock also capture nitrogen or other useful gasses?

The refinery equipment rumbled in the background. His ear protection implants apparently couldn't tell whether to block it, so he'd been subjected to a maddening intermittent buzzing for the last four hours. "Were you ever assigned to work in here?"

He gathered the refinery shut down processing operations the moment the blowout alarm sounded. Everyone in the refinery had heard the echoing announcement telling the refinery workers to stay at their workstation until further notice. Like they had a choice.

"Yeah, right after I was captured. Then a Volksstam prisoner got caught using the refinery's transport system to secretly direct some gravity-plate bots to excavate toward the visitor's ship hangar instead of following the ore seam. The warden decided all pirate clan scum were a flight risk and removed us well away from anything that put us near the surface or anything important." Her electric-blue eyes flashed with annoyance. "*Beschaafd* assholes probably believe their own scare-mongering and think we can teleport."

He'd always thought *beschaafd* meant "civilized" in Dutch, but not the way she used it. Something to ask her later. Right now, he had survival questions to ask. "How do the griffins stay alive?"

"It's a mystery from the Chaos God of Dark Energy to keep us entertained." A crooked smile flitted across her face. "Or to piss off the red-robed twist. He detests them."

From what Zade had overheard during meals, the prisoners had dozens of nicknames for the warden. As if saying his name would conjure him.

Julke flexed one foot, toe forward, then the other. "Sutrio's best guess is that decades ago, someone on the mine staff was also a freelance genetic designer working on new griffin species to sell to the pet trade. The designer is long gone, but the asteroid now has four species of feral griffins that can thrive in an oxygen-poor, dust-rich environment. All they need is humans to bring food, water, insects, and vermin."

"What's the fourth species?"

"Rock griffins. Very pale. Big eyes, bigger claws, and a barbed tail for hanging on rocks. They live in the Abyss."

"Hmm." He affected a prissy, condescending tone. "Must be another attraction the orientation vids neglected to mention."

Her eyebrow twitched in wry amusement. "It's a huge fissure inside the asteroid. Looks like someone once tried to enclose part of it. Multiple trails of miner-type gravity plates with built-in perpetual lights that lead nowhere. These days, it's mostly a dump pit for trash tailings and non-recyclables." She drew her knees closer and rested her elbows on them.

"How big is 'huge'? Is it close to the surface like the refinery?"

"No idea." She shook her head. "I've only been there twice. It's darker than deep space where the lights can't reach. Oxygen and humidity levels fluctuate with the wind. Which shouldn't be possible, but enough for the rock griffins to breathe and fly. The guards swear they've seen little explosions."

"Explosions, like blowouts?" That sounded dangerous. Escape routes were only good if they didn't kill the escapees.

"Who knows? Scares the daylights out of them, that's

for sure." Her mouth twisted in a rueful smile. "They're even more superstitious than the Volksstam."

A hamstring pinch in his right thigh made him separate and splay his feet. The stretch of spreading his heels out wide and leaning over to touch his elbows felt good. Or at least better than before. For all that his life seemed to involve running from one thing and another, he hated the actual activity.

"You're very flexible," she murmured.

"Born that way." He twisted at the waist to hover over his right knee. The impulse to show off made him conscious of a desire to impress her as much as she impressed him.

She snorted. "I was born short."

He turned his head up to give her a crooked smile. "Short people don't whack their heads on hopper maintenance doors nearly as often."

A pulse of laughter escaped her. "Good point."

Lantham snorted in his sleep and scratched at his nose.

Zade darted glances at Sutrio, nearby prisoners, and the guards. No one seemed to be awake or remotely interested in their conversation.

Nonetheless, the last thing he wanted to do was to irritate Julke. He was aware he talked too much. "Worse than a therapist's AI," as a previous drunken crewmate had described it, right before nailing him with a shockstick.

He sat upright, then rolled down to lie on his back and gaze at the ceiling, one hand resting on his diaphragm, the other arm cradling his head to protect his scalp from the cold floor, since his hair was growing back too slowly to do any good. He firmly ignored the new questions bubbling in his head, such as how many meters the refinery was from the asteroid's surface, or how close they were to the landing zone. If he kept his eyes on the shadows, maybe he'd see a draco griffin.

"You don't have to answer this," said Julke quietly, "but how did you get caught?"

He glanced at her, but she was bent over her knee, fiddling with her boot, so he couldn't see her expression. Her emotions hinted at the briny taste of loneliness and the tannin taste of remorse before he contained his wayward talent. That kind of prying wasn't the way to treat friends. Especially since it made him want to offer to hold and comfort her, and never let her go. Empaths were susceptible to touch starvation.

"Desperation. My former crew wanted to use what I have or sell it. I chose option three and jumped ship at the next space station. I took the next gig I could find. Should have looked a little closer." The admission was out before it occurred to him to hide his stupidity. He blew out a noisy breath. "Knowing Captain Fazhian, they're still scouring the galaxy for me. She doesn't like to be crossed."

"What do you have?" The tone was gentle, inviting.

His rational brain told him to deflect like always, but heart told him to trust her. The universe wasn't just a collection of meaningless random events. He had to believe the compatible mesh of their empathy was more than just luck.

"A... talent. Maybe." Describing it turned out to be harder than he thought. "The Citizen Protection Service doesn't list it in their official classes or categories." He sat up again, then twisted slowly toward her and back in a slow-motion stretch. "I can make people want to like me. Trust me. Even shielders, if they're not on alert."

He hesitated, then decided to tell her the rest. In for a micron, in for a meter, as his engineering instructor used to say.

"I don't use my... whatever-it-is often, but I foolishly pushed it hard to get me and some shipmates out of a trade deal about to go fatally twisted. One of them told Fazhian. She promised to make me wealthy if I used it to benefit her. When I didn't jump at the chance, she made it clear that if I didn't cooperate, she'd sell me to the Citizen Protection Service. They pay bounties for uniques. No one knows what happens to the CPS recruits."

The only sign she heard him was her fingers paused in their fidgeting for several long moments. "The CPS are void-brains. My people call it *bekorensgave*. The gift of charm."

It was oddly comforting to know it had a name. That meant his talent was real, at least to the Volksstam, and not just a defect to be dissected. Maybe whoever had abandoned him at the medical center as a baby had Volksstam heritage.

"We also have *negerensgave*. To make people ignore things that are right in front of them."

Something in her words made him glance at her.

"You?" He found it hard enough to even look away from her, much less ignore her. She lit up a room without even trying.

His skepticism must have shown on his face. With a subtle pulse, her empath talent lightly brushed his, then skittered away like a griffin in flight, leading his full attention upward.

Stunned, he caught himself blinking in surprise. If she seriously activated, he bet she could have picked every pocket he had and walked out the door before he noticed.

"Brilliant," he murmured, meaning it. That kind of talent could have gotten him out of parsecs of trouble. The more he learned about her, the more he wanted to know. "How did they catch you?"

Despite his containment, he sensed a flurry of emotions from her before she bottled them up. "Betrayal." Her jaw tightened briefly. "I have time-sensitive information my people need. A former lover was sent to kill me to shut me up, but he sent me here instead. I'd like to think he didn't know it's a one-way trip."

Disparate facts about her clicked together in a pattern. Every trade representative he'd ever met was part diplomat, part info broker, and part spy. Why should the Volksstam be any different? "Politics?"

"Yes." Her eyes flashed in challenge. "You know there's big trouble coming, right?"

"Yes." It was a relief to find someone else who recognized it. "I don't know if your people have heard of the Ayorinn's Legacy prophecy about freedom for minders, but it terrifies the Citizen Protection Service. It's flared up again and again over the years, and lately, it's in every other planetary newstrend. I think the CPS would destroy just about anything to stop it." His chest felt tight. "But the rest of the galaxy is in deep denial. If you want to start a fight, stand up in a pub and tell them that the Concordance isn't too big to fail, and that two hundred years of peace don't mean jack shit when it comes to predicting the future." Shaking his head, he sighed. "It's not going to go well."

"True." A hint of sadness flitted across her face. "Our leaders know about the Legacy, and we track the news, but they think it doesn't apply to them. I'm not so sure. The Volksstam are splintering. Some *familiestams* want to move beyond the galactic frontier and wait for the CGC to burn. Others want to light the fuse so they can claim everything not tied down, *then* move to the frontier. And some want to help the non-combatants survive the conflagration and rebuild because the universe is unforgiving and we need each other."

His talent detected the anise flavor of determination when she mentioned the third option.

An earsplitting clatter of multi-band static suddenly boomed and echoed through the facility. It stuttered like a faulty comm system, then went silent. Or maybe that was his implants interfering. The medics told him they'd only left them operational because he didn't have a controller. Otherwise, they'd have had to keep him offline another day while they removed it. Another of the warden's weird little rules, like forbidding autonomous AIs from running anything, meaning human staff had to do it.

Whatever the sound was, it was enough to wake some of the prisoners, including Sutrio and Lantham.

Zade watched the guards have an animated discussion, pointing toward the lifts and sealed blast doors. Four of the guards fanned out among the prisoners.

A few moments later, Lhap Cho, the guard who'd been assigned to their shift, approached their group. He checked off each of their names on his tablet. The man looked tired. No naps for the guards.

Taking a chance that Lhap Cho wasn't shielding tightly, Zade sent a slender thread of his *bekoren* talent. "Any news from Admin?"

Lhap Cho shook his head. "They're still checking the damage. And looking for signals again."

Zade assumed an earnest, innocent look. "Signals?" He pushed again with his talent.

Lhap Cho rolled his eyes. "Like the static feedback we just heard. Security has had a bug up their butt for weeks about phantom outside comms signals. They've been sending bots rigged with scanners to all the old work areas looking for it, then making us personally check out any anomalies." His tone said he didn't think much of the task.

Zade gave him a crooked smile. "In your abundant free time, of course."

"Of course." Lhap Cho chuckled. "Let me know if you come across any exploration comms beacons when you're digging chofi."

Unexpectedly, he felt a sharp taste of interest from Julke, quickly contained. He coughed to disguise his surprise.

After Lhap Cho stepped away toward the next group, Sutrio sat up and stretched. "I wouldn't put it past them to blame the griffins."

Julke stifled a laugh. "Right. Couldn't possibly be that the mine's tech was old when the CGC toppled the Central League two hundred years ago, or their maps are full of holes."

Nodding, Sutrio added, "Or that because the staff drove griffins out of their areas, the rats and insects have free rein. Probably chewed through something vital, and now the paranoid top asshole has his whole operation chasing stellar reflection echoes." She took a quick sip of water from her suit's tube. They'd be needing refills soon. Perspiration and humidity from their breath were leaking into the dry refinery air instead of recycled by their suits.

Zade caught Sutrio's eye. "Do the griffins talk to each other?"

"Sure," she said. "They're socially cooperative, like birds. I think some of them are telepathic among themselves, and maybe with humans. If so, they're probably more valuable than the fucking rocks."

Julke nodded. "I believe it." She tilted her head. "Long-timer tales said the prisoners used to have them carry messages. Of course, the guards' literal-minded solution was to take away anything for prisoners to write with or on."

"Hmph," said Zade. "Mix chofi dust with saliva or sweat and you could write on any surface. Look at the indelible spots in the decontamination zone." He smiled. "It'd make a great colorant for printing parts, except for its unfortunate tendency to explode."

Lantham shook his head. "It's more stable than organic substrates, especially once it's shaped. Makes the strongest incalloy, but it's rare and expensive." He patted the floor. "It's so plentiful here, they use it to make gravity plates. I bet we're sitting on enough chofirium-based incalloy to armor a fleet of military ships. Good engineering, though. If a blowout happens here, the energy will radiate out into space, not downward where the valuables are."

Zade thought about it for a moment. "Makes sense. They probably did the same for the ship hangars and the landing field." Which reminded him of a question he'd been saving for a relatively private moment like this. "Where in the galaxy are we, anyway?"

Sutrio looked down. Lantham rolled over and turned his back to Zade. Belatedly, his talent tasted the acid of their ire.

"Shut it." Julke's mouth tightened. "Unless you want to be worse than dead, don't even *think* about that. The warden has telepaths. I'm not telling you again. He'd kill everyone on this asteroid to keep the location secret."

Her hissed words stung. "What's worse than dead?"

"Leashed with a lethal analog collar, like the warden's personal protectors." She pointed a trigger finger at her temple. "Brain-wiped and sealed in a red-armored mech suit so you can become a warden's guardian. Or maybe they'll give us to the pharma researchers for vivisection."

He hadn't expected their reaction. "Sorry."

"You're not." He felt Julke's acidic anger turn to milky resignation as she sighed and rested her chin on her forearm. "We're screwed."

Sutrio grunted. "The warden eats glitterball noobs for breakfast. We'll just be collateral damage for whatever they do to you." She rubbed the back of her neck. "If you won't learn from the smartest prisoner in the mine" — she tilted her chin toward Julke — "learn from the griffins." She stood to stretch, then lay down on the floor even farther from him than before.

Conflict spiked his stress level to the stratosphere, but it was his own farking fault. He made himself sit and think instead of moving to another group that wasn't mad at him.

Julke was right. He wasn't sorry he'd asked the question, but he'd forgotten to be discreet. Considering that's what betrayed him to his former crew, he'd have thought he'd learned that lesson.

Sutrio was right, too. They didn't know he was telepath immune, but if he got caught, the warden wouldn't believe he'd acted alone. Griffins didn't stomp in and steal in broad daylight they waited and snuck in when no one was looking. And they cooperated with each other and with humans.

He had to admit he tanked at that. All he'd wanted was acceptance and a challenge or two, but he'd made increasingly dubious choices in outfits to work for. It made him good at escaping trouble, but he always ended up alone, starting over. He'd hoped his new course would have changed that. Then Nova Nine happened.

Pushing past his hurt, he mirrored Julke's position, which put his head closer to hers. "I really am sorry." He kept his voice as low as he could, and relaxed his containment so she could feel his sincerity. "I want all of us free, not just me."

She tilted her head to look at him but said nothing.

"My former captain is an obsessed, vengeful asshole, but she's galaxy class at tracking hidden treasure and people she wants to kill. Nova Nine now has both." He dragged a finger through the dust on the floor, sketching the official symbol for the Central Galactic Concordance's galactic communication system. "If she received a traceable comm, she could bring a fleet."

Julke's long, still silence began to worry him. Had he made another terrible mistake?

"Interesting, but not much of a solution if you're dead." Her soft tone sounded skeptical, but his talent caught a brief flavor of concern.

He disguised his relief with a shrug. "She'd have to catch me first. But in the meantime, she'd crack this place open like a shiny geode. Particular enemies excepted" — he waved a thumb toward his chest — "she hates kidnapping and slavery."

Julke's lips thinned. "Assuming she doesn't accidentally blow up the whole asteroid, Nova Nine has defenses." She sighed again. "I shouldn't be telling you this because it'll give you ideas. The mine has hidden energy guns and ship killers, old and new. Probably more that the guards don't gripe about. And thanks to the xeronium we mine and refine, almost limitless energy to power them. She wouldn't stand a chance."

"She might if she knew what she's up against. Jackers might sell everything else, but they keep armor and weapons for themselves. They out-gun CGC's Space Div frontier patrols."

"Why are you telling me this?"

He opened his mouth to speak, then stopped. It wouldn't help his case to admit he tanked at making life choices, or that she inspired him to want to make better ones.

Corralling his thoughts, he tried again. "I've felt more at home here than I have in the last decade of being on any ship's crew. It doesn't hurt that I don't have to hide being a minder. But it's more than that. The prisoners squabble, and some are hard cases, but they look out for one another. Everyone listens to you, and they listen to Sutrio about the griffins because you do. And Lantham about materials. And Prughal about how to operate the work area enviro units. I could name others. Even some of the guards listen to you." He caught her gaze. "The only way out of here is working together."

Her fingers twitched as her face scrunched in thought. Finally she shook her head. "I'm a *reiziger* among my people. I'm no leader."

"Aren't you? I don't know what 'traveler' means to the Volksstam, but you're more than that here. You know everyone, even the three noobs I was caught with. Not as just a list of memorized names, but the individuals as people. The prisoners come to you. I've seen them at mealtimes."

She blew out an exasperated breath. "Arbitrating arguments is not the same–"

The mine's attention tone sounded throughout the facility.

"All clear. Return to assigned work areas. Clear the blast door thresholds. Refinery will begin operation in fifteen minutes."

The guards stepped into and sealed their mech suits, then moved toward the prisoners. Lhap Cho strode toward their group.

Zade had already taken a cue from the other prisoners and was just sealing his helmet when Lhap Cho arrived.

"Lantham, Sutrio, go with Workgroup 23-A and work

with them the rest of the shift." He turned to Julke. "You and Lunaso, come with me."

Zade didn't bother looking at Julke's expression to see if this was usual. His talent picked up on both her consternation and the edges of Lhap Cho's irritation.

He kept a tight rein on the chilling dread that his earlier questions had brought both him and Julke to the attention of the warden's interrogators.

6

NOVA NINE FACILITY • GDAT 3243.117

J ulke felt Zade fight to contain his alarm as they followed Lhap Cho. If they were in trouble, she deserved the mega-share of the blame. She'd known Zade was too tempting to talk to, and felt remorse for crushing his dreams of escape.

However, Lhap Cho would have shackled them if they were headed to the punishment block. Instead, he led them to the lifts and entered a code to call a capsule. When the doors opened almost immediately, he ushered them inside, then stepped in himself.

"Hey, Lunaso," he said with an overly cheery demeanor, "any experience in caves?"

Julke had a sinking feeling she knew where they were going.

"No. Some derelict recovery, though." Zade's voice was nonchalant.

Lhap Cho laughed. "Oh, is that what you space jackers are calling slice-and-hauls these days?"

Zade shrugged, his equanimity unruffled.

Lhap Cho chuckled again. "That'll do. Admin thinks they've identified an old comms system in the Abyss. I'll set an anchor at the access point and send you two out with a scanner to get readings."

Thanks to Zade's earlier use of his talent, she knew they were looking for something a lot bigger than a few old control nodes or exposed cables.

"What's the Abyss?" Zade excelled at sounding innocent.

"Big fucking hole." Lhap Cho's voice seemed tighter than usual. "You'll see." A tinge of trepidation slipped past the guard's habitual shield.

Not that she blamed him. She didn't like the Abyss, either. The impossible winds felt too much like melancholic death ghosts who wanted her to join their ranks.

Zade, on the other hand, was barely containing his flare of curiosity. The man was more hopeful than an adventurous griffin, poking his beak into everything in case it turned out to be something edible.

Surviving another close call had made her realize they all might die before she even had the chance to explore the potential connection with Zade. Or to share a stolen kiss with him and ask if he wanted more. Somehow, in the last few hours, his irrepressible optimism had infected her. Waiting for the perfect opportunity hadn't been working, so why not try the less perfect options?

Nova Nine might be killing her by centimeters, but she wasn't dead yet. She wasn't the leader Zade seemed to think, but damnit, she was Volksstam, not some soft CGC citizen on a fat planet waiting for another handout. She'd taken over maintaining the prisoner network from the Volksstam prisoner who'd looked out for her when she was a noob. Plus, she had resources and talents the greedy ghoul in red and his minions never dreamed of. It was about time she used them.

THEIR ENTRY into the Abyss turned out to be through a temporary double airlock erected over a new jagged hole in an old corkscrew-shaped tunnel. She knew the tunnel was old because previous practice had been to smooth the dead rock walls after ore extraction, which left little dust. Nowadays, with water more plentiful, they didn't bother.

Thanks to her filer memory, she would remember the route to the breach, but she didn't have enough reference points to make her own map.

Lhap Cho anchored both her and Zade to the wall via monofibre cables that would slice through exosuits and their waists before breaking. He also supplied gravity boots, lights, and tethered cameras that sent a feed to Lhap Cho's controller. Zade got some light climbing gear, and she got the comms scanner.

"Lunaso, you go first." He opened the first airlock door and motioned Zade through. "Don't trust the warped gravity plate on the left. It took out our flying camera." The first door irised shut.

Zade nodded and gave a thumbs-up sign, then stepped into the darkness after the second door opened.

When Lhap Cho motioned her through, she told

herself it was an ordinary walk in space, just like exosuits were designed to handle.

Her eyes needed several moments to adapt to the dark. The phantom lights she remembered seemed more plentiful in this area. Too easy to imagine they were stress fractures in an old ship's hull. Focusing on Zade's broad shoulders helped. She let herself find comfort in his emotional strength.

Zade keyed the light on his shoulder and aimed it to the right. The gravity plate beneath them curved ninety degrees up and more to the right. It connected to a twisting path of more gravity plates.

She pointed her own light to the left. The next gravity plate over looked like a torn tissue with a gaping black void between it and a farther row of plates. Even as she watched, dust whirled across her light's beam. Lhap Cho would never see his camera again.

"Go right about five sections," ordered Lhap Cho, *"then run the scanner."*

The capricious winds pummeled them with dust and pebbles as they cautiously made their way along the metal path. The old-style plates only had embedded surface lights, not the pillar lights they now incorporated. The walkway followed the convoluted contour of the rock wall. No landmarks meant she was completely lost by the third twist. Their safety lines were their only way back to the airlock.

Her imagination supplied the howling sounds, even though her suit blocked the noise. She worried that Zade's larger profile would make him more vulnerable to the gusts. Narrowing her focus to each step she took helped keep her brain occupied and fear at bay.

At the fifth plate, she gratefully hunkered down with the scanner. In the distance, a flattened sphere of small blue lights up and left seemed to be hovering in space. It looked familiar, but she couldn't place it. Something someone described to her, maybe? She'd need quiet time to search her filer memory for the reference.

"Lunaso, I can't see shit on your camera," complained Lhap Cho. *"Is it still on?"*

Zade tapped the camera with his gloved finger. "It's green go."

"What about the scanner? I'm not getting that feed, either."

Julke checked the controls. "It's activated. It's seeing our comms."

It took her a second glance to realize it had been set to look for too narrow a wavelength band. They could be standing on top of a fully operational galactic comms relay and the scanner wouldn't detect it. If she'd needed another nudge from the gods, there it was.

After another twenty minutes of navigating the twisting plates and getting no results, Lhap Cho ordered them to wait while he spoke to the techs.

Instead of hugging the wall to avoid the winds, Zade stepped toward the black void and dropped to one knee at the edge of the plate.

Julke wanted to look away, but she didn't dare, in case she had to reel him in. The Abyss seemed like it wanted to play with its victims. Well, too damn bad. The guards had given him to her, and she was keeping him.

Zade waved to get her attention, then gave her the sign for griffin plus a waving motion she couldn't interpret. Lip-reading wasn't her gift. She shook her head and shrugged to tell him she had no idea what he was saying.

He stood and backed up a couple of steps, then dropped to his knees and sat on his heels. He almost looked meditative, but his *bekorensgave* talent blazed to life. It wasn't directed at her.

In seconds, something white and fast swooped in and out of the light. Two more sped by. This time, she got a glimpse of wings. Rock griffins.

Soon they were surrounded by a flurry of griffins. One landed in front of Zade's knees. He looked down. She didn't need to see his face to feel his joy and wonder.

She'd never met a *bekorensgave* minder who could affect animals, but only the CGC's benighted Citizen Protection Service pretended they knew everything about minder talents. The Volksstam would welcome him with open arms. Or at least she would.

Daydreaming wasn't helping. She should be taking advantage of her god-gifted opportunity instead. She set the scanner down, then sat cross-legged behind it. The readout on her oxy concentrator said the external air had too little oxygen to breathe, but it wouldn't kill her. Focusing, she took several big gulps of air to charge her lungs. Then she took a normal breath and held it while she quickly opened her helmet and removed her gloves.

The flock of vocalizing rock griffins sounded like cyclonic winds. Bitter cold shocked her eyes as she quickly slid her little fingers under her braids. When she located the tiny lumps just above and behind both ears, she pressed the complex sequential pattern. Ice stung her nostrils and froze her eyelashes.

As she sealed her helmet again and gulped air, the Volksstam-style bio-controller in her head woke up. With no time to waste, she closed her eyes and queried all the bands the CGC had ever used for intergalactic communications.

And there it was. A vintage exploration comms relay. From the ping-back, it was a configuration her people had hacked long ago. The signal was strong enough that it had to originate somewhere in the asteroid. Taking the chance while she had it, she used memorized backdoor codes to query the relay for a diagnostic dump, committed every datapoint to memory, then immediately closed her connection. The scanner in front of her remained blissfully quiet, but others in the mine's security center might notice the activity. She hoped the traffic would get lost in the sea of anomalies that had sparked their current investigation in the first place.

Her head swam with the masses of numbers swirling in her thoughts. It would take days to sort them. She'd have to disable her bio-controller later. As it was, her achingly cold, stiff hands made it a struggle to pull on and reattach her gloves.

A new voice came online. *"Defayensdytr, check the scanner and tell me what you see."* It sounded like Halool, one of the facility techs.

Julke adjusted her light so she could see the display better. "Our comms, plus a two-second blip."

"Why do I have to do everything myself?" said Halool.

"The blip should be the camera. Power it down and up again."

Zade, surrounded by griffins, rose to his feet and made shooing motions with his hands. The griffins seemed to think it was a game to dodge his hands and land on his arms or shoulders. There had to be at least fifteen of them. One landed on his helmet, making him look like an avian alien invader from an adventure serial.

Thinking fast, Julke spoke out loud. "Lunaso can't get to the cable. I'll have to unhook it from his shoulder. Do you want a panorama of the Abyss?"

"Yes." Lhap Cho.

She pointed to all the griffins, then used sign language and waving motions to tell him to convince them to move back behind him.

He nodded and stepped back. With another wave of his *bekorensgave,* the griffins followed as if basking in sunlight. Julke was hard pressed not to laugh as two of them played tug of war with his safety line and three rode his boot like they were children.

When the griffins were crowded against the wall, he stepped in front of them. They seemed content to stay where they were. He coaxed the helmet-riding griffin onto his arm, where it wrapped itself around his forearm like living jewelry.

She crossed to him quickly and unplugged the camera, put it on her shoulder, then plugged it back into the power source belted to his waist. She took a deep, calming breath, then turned and stepped closer to the edge of the plate so the camera had a clear view of the Abyss.

"How's that?" The distant lights seemed to jitter. She tblinked her eyes several times hard.

"Good," said Lhap Cho. *"Sweep in horizontal rows, left to right."*

She did as ordered, watching to make sure she didn't catch any griffins in flight. Behind her, Zade continued broadcasting his amazing talent. It made *her* want to get skin-to-skin close to him, and she wasn't even a griffin.

When the sphere of blue lights came into frame, Lhap Cho ordered her to stop. *"What's that?"*

"Zoom in," said Halool. *"Defayensdytr, can you get closer?"*

"No." To forestall any arguments, Julke rotated the camera and her light down toward her feet to show where the plate ended. She was sorry she did so, because as far as she could tell, the plate was hanging in midair. *Just like a spacewalk*, she told herself.

"It's not our target. We'll look at the vids later." Bless Lhap Cho for his focus. *"Defayensdytr, get the rest of the coverage. Come back to the airlock when you're done."*

As she swung the camera back toward the Abyss, it suddenly hit Julke what the blue lights were. When she'd first arrived, one of the long-timer Volksstam prisoners had gifted her with a legacy packet of collected Volksstam memories to help her survive. She hadn't needed to access it in a long time. The lights marked a back entrance to the warden's personal ship hangar.

By itself, the fact was useless. They'd need a spaceworthy ship just to cross the Abyss. But with that memory came another, of a detailed navigator-style holo map that included the prisoner cells, the various staff offices, and the executive suite. Most importantly, it covered the front entrance to the warden's private hangar. The gifted memory felt decades old, and some of the map was outdated. The pharma company now occupied what had once been the prisoner area. Several former excavation tunnels now housed the new prison cell blocks. No telling what changes had been made to the staff areas since.

However, the current warden struck her as the type to have multiple ways to save his red-robed rump. Such as a well-armored transit-capable starship, primed and ready to launch at a moment's notice. They wouldn't need Zade's distraction if they could get to it, and no one would shoot it down if they thought Kanogan was piloting. Then they could go for help to rescue all the prisoners.

Too many unknowns to track down by herself. Didn't want to do it alone, either. When she'd been younger, she might have believed she was the only person who could save them all. Real life had knocked some sense into her.

And if Nova Nine had taught her nothing else, it was like Zade said: Working together was their best shot. His *bekorensgave* talent gave him an edge in ferreting out vital information. But she'd have to make sure the man understood what he was risking.

To pull off an escape, many things had to go miraculously right. Even so, this moment in the shattering Abyss felt like the closest to freedom she'd been in five hundred days.

7

NOVA NINE FACILITY • GDAT 3243.120

Z ade shuffled along at the end of the slow-moving queue of prisoners toward the food service counters. He was too brain-dead to remember the names of the prisoners in front of him, and too tired to look at their nametags. They didn't seem inclined to look at his, either. Exhaustion had a way of killing conviviality.

Was it good or bad that he couldn't smell anything over the sour scent of his own body? Chem showers every five days never seemed to do the job. His lower back was mad about working debris cleanup for the whole shift with a new workgroup that didn't trust the noob. Clamping down his empathic talent to protect himself from the crowd was giving him a headache.

The mine had reorganized the shift schedule since losing six prisoners, a guard, and a bunch of equipment to the blowout three days ago. Consequently, the remaining prisoners were working fifteen-hour shifts with reconfigured workgroups and unfamiliar equipment. And currently crammed into the dining hall all at once.

That might be why the mine temporarily resorted to handing out emergency-ration mealpacks. A lot quicker to serve than fresh-cooked food from the asteroid's hydroponic farm. Mealpack flavors and textures were rarely pleasant, but they didn't throw his digestive system off kilter, either.

Mealtimes used to mean social time with Julke, but she'd sent him on a mission. Something had changed in her since blowout day. She seemed more engaged. Even lugubrious Lantham had commented. Zade counted himself lucky the mine still considered him Julke's trainee and hadn't separated them.

His brief time in the Abyss had changed him, too. The big void intrigued him. Instincts honed by a lifetime of getting out of sticky situations told him it was important.

The rock griffins amazed him. He'd actually seen flickering alien images in his mind and felt mercurial emotions. It was the closest he'd probably ever come to knowing what telepathy felt like.

He longed to try his talent on the common griffins in the human habitation area, but he didn't dare. If they came to him, they'd be easy targets for trigger-happy dolts like Dajoya.

And none of it would have happened without Julke. Despite her palpable terror of the Abyss, she'd given him the space to try his "charm gift" talent on the griffins. Plus covered for him when it worked better than he'd ever imagined. The least he could do in return was ferret out information for her. He'd been doing his own data gathering, anyway. It didn't matter that she hadn't told him why she wanted it. It was enough for him that she did.

He took the mealpack and water pouch from the stacks and clutched them close as he left the counter area, evaluating the open spaces.

As always, his eyes looked for Julke. She was sitting in the middle of a long table, mealpack in front of her, and interacting with a couple of the long-timer prisoners. One of them he knew to be Volksstam.

His feet wanted to take him to her. He knew next to nothing about her people and wanted to learn more. The CGC entertainment industry romanticized them for profit but kept the insulting name. Indie traders and freight haulers hated them as thieves, and jackers hated the competition. CGC military leaders scapegoated the pirate clan, much like Nova Nine's guards blamed the griffins for everything. The truth was likely much more fascinating.

Resolutely, he turned away and chose a table on the other side of the hall near a corner. He was one of the last to sit, after sliding down the bench to make sure he could see Julke. He'd never seen another prisoner bother her, but he wanted to be aware if someone tried. If his luck held, the crowd would thin out and he could start a casual chat with—

Three long alert tones reverberated in the hall, bringing all conversion to a halt. A flash flood of the bitter lavender of fear threatened to overwhelm his containment. The prisoners set down their utensils. Kitchen staff and guards stood ramrod straight. All heads turned toward the hall's sets of double doors.

A moment later, they irised open all at once.

Two warden's guardians in red mech suits marched in

and took positions near the doors. Their blank expressions matched their uncanny stillness once they stopped.

Seven enforcers in gold tunics and black pants and boots followed. They fanned out in between the rows of tables stood, eyes flicking to every movement from the prisoners.

Kanogan strode into the room and stopped in the center of the traffic area, feet apart, fists on his hips. The enveloping red robe's fluttering hem pooled around his feet. The distortion hood made his face unreadable, but his body language said he enjoyed being the center of attention.

Two more gold-and-black uniforms stationed themselves on either side of the warden, one pace behind. Protectors, the other prisoners had called them. Rumor said the thick collars they each wore would instantly kill the wearer if they got too far from Kanogan.

The last three people to enter walked in with casual confidence that bordered on arrogance. The diagonal red sashes they wore matched the color of the warden's flowing purity cloak. The extra spike of fear in the room confirmed Zade's impression they were likely the warden's infamous elite interrogation team. He clamped down hard on his empath talent and put a dull expression on his face. Nothing to see and no one of interest in his corner of the hall.

After a moment of silence, Kanogan spoke. "I have some announcements, but first, it has come to my attention that we have a star in our midst who has been hiding his light." His amplified voice sounded warm, almost playful. "Mr. Waorani, please stand up. Don't be shy."

Zade froze, striving to keep as still as a stealth griffin. Waorani had been the tattooed man in the group he'd been caught with in the space station. The other two recruits had died in the blowout, leaving only himself and Waorani as the last noobs.

When no one stood, two enforcers converged on the man and forced him to stand, tightly gripping his arms. Zade was only one table away. The man's fear and rage pounded against Zade's containment, demanding to be acknowledged.

Kanogan continued expansively. "Mr. Waorani is a sifter, but he modestly claimed only a low-level talent. A little bird told us he's actually top-level, and CPS Institute trained." He waved both gloved hands in presentation style. "Congratulations! I'm promoting you to my staff."

"I refuse." Waorani's forceful words echoed off the walls.

Kanogan's head turned toward Waorani. "Well, that's unexpected. Most new prisoners jump at the chance." He sounded like a teacher disappointed in a student. "Perhaps we can change your mind."

The two enforcers dragged Waorani out from the tables and forced him to kneel several meters before Kanogan. From Zade's vantage point, all he could see was Waorani's head and shoulders.

The warden gestured. The interrogators stepped forward. One closed her eyes.

Waorani surged to his feet with a roar. Enforcers and interrogators stumbled back as if pushed by an explosion.

Kanogan's two protectors dragged him sideways, toward the doors.

An interrogator regained her footing. "Shut him down!" A heartbeat later, she was thrown backward and slammed into one of the red-armored hulks, knocking them both off their feet.

Waorani roared. The other interrogators went flying again.

Kanogan's voice boomed. "Red Team, disable Waorani 3006."

The still-standing guardian stepped forward. An invisible wind slid her backward. In answer, she deployed ground spikes, making holes in the metal floor with each step toward her target. The second prime guard crawled in the same direction. The chair that slid into him didn't slow his advance.

Waorani fell to one knee. "I... will... not... submit!"

Suddenly he arched and jerked, then slumped and toppled.

Zade couldn't see why until one of the enforcers climbed to her feet, holding a slender shockstick. He recognized it as the same style Kanogan had hit him with the first day.

"Red Team, stand down. Return to position one." Kanogan stepped forward, shrugging off the hand of one of his protectors. His head turned toward the enforcer with the shockstick. "Well done. Perhaps the rest of my staff can learn to be as quick-thinking."

He turned to the interrogators, who were helping each other up off the floor. "Regrettably, Mr. Waorani turns out to be too volatile to join my personal staff. Telekinetics are intractable liars. Clean him out and take him to processing. Red Team can always use fresh meat."

The interrogation team enlisted one of the enforcers to help put Waorani's inert form in a wheeled cart and rolled it out the door. The Red Team guards resumed their positions, as did the protectors and remaining enforcers.

Kanogan turned to face the prisoner population. "I'd planned that as a celebration, but..." He trailed off, then shrugged and waved a gloved hand. "On to the announcements. I appreciate the extra hours you've all put in these last three days. Thanks to you, we've already exceeded this quarter's production goals. That's a big win for our little operation." He paused as if expecting a round of applause.

From what Zade could see, the other prisoners looked as stunned as he felt. Despite his tight containment, he sensed consternation and disgust from the people around him. Phantom spots danced in his peripheral vision as his headache veered into migraine territory. He couldn't tell if Kanogan actually believed his own words, or was playing a twisted game of pretending the prisoners were willing employees.

"Anyway," continued Kanogan, "the good news is, we're expecting an influx of people and equipment in seven or eight days. We'll have to keep the longer shifts until then, but we've reactivated some older extraction equipment so you can return to the previous work detail assignments. We need to keep the momentum going. More output is the key to expanding our customer base."

Zade darted quick glances at the warden's staff for

reactions to the bizarre motivational speech, but they were nearly as statue-faced as the guardians.

"I saved the best for last." Kanogan's over-the-top energetic enthusiasm would have instilled begrudging envy in a used-starship dealer. "As a reward for your efforts, starting tonight, I've authorized one extra hour of sleep!"

He opened his arms wide to accept applause. None came. The room descended into a long, awkward silence.

An audible huff came over the speakers. "Very well, then." His arms dropped and his head lifted. "Enjoy your dinner." The suddenly snappish tone said he hoped they choked.

Kanogan turned with a flurry of red and headed straight for the doors.

It took a second for the enforcers to realize their boss was actually leaving. A couple had to trot to catch up to the retinue as they exited.

Zade waited until he saw Julke relax before allowing himself to slump and release the screaming tension in his back. It even hurt to lift his arms to trigger the heater in his mealpack and unpack the recyclable utensils. The pent-up emotions in the hall buffeted his talent. Letting his head drop to his chest, he visualized hand-weaving a basket to reassemble his tattered containment.

He owed Julke an apology for disbelieving her about how the Red Team guards were recruited. It was worse even than court-ordered punishment for the CGC's most heinous criminals. "Cleaner" was a slang term for a particular type of telepath who could erase memories as if they never existed. Everything that was uniquely Waorani would be gone.

The mealpack's steam-release signaled the contents were ready to eat. He pried off the top and began methodically shoveling mystery lumps of moist green protein from the tray to his mouth. The best he could say about the taste was that he'd had worse.

The bone-thin prisoner across the table, whose name tag Zade couldn't read shook his head. "How can you eat this shit, Lunaso?"

Zade shrugged one shoulder. "Not in favor of starving."

Prughal, the gold-haired prisoner next to him, grunted. "Better get used to it. Guards were bitching about having to clean out frost damage in the hydroponics farm. Blowout made a big hole in the ceiling."

"It didn't freeze?" Zade looked at Prughal in surprise.

"Dunno." Prughal ate another spoonful of something yellow and grainy. "Maybe it wasn't hard vacuum. In any case, it'll take 'em days just to re-start the plankton colonies."

Zade recalled that Prughal was a plant affinity minder with closed enviro systems expertise. Not that the mine would trust a prisoner anywhere near critical infrastructure, but what a waste to have such a clever person drilling holes in rocks.

Judging from the emotional flavors of the room, no one would be inclined to make small talk, much less tell him the things he needed to know. In the meantime, the narrow sleep shelf in his cell was calling his name.

8

Julke straightened her pillow, then turned over on the narrow bed, away from the faint lights, and rearranged the blanket so it was even and just skimmed her shoulder. The cells were cool but not cold. Like most prisoners, she slept in her clothes so she'd have a few extra minutes of sleep in the morning.

Considering how long she'd been awake, she was going to need it. She was losing time in every way that mattered. Memories of Waorani's defeat and its devastating effect on the prisoners tangled with dark visions of what the warden's sadistic elite interrogators would do to the man. She'd been close enough to feel their sadistic glee. They'd want him awake, helpless, and aware of his destruction.

In the cell behind her, Lantham snored. No sound came from Sutrio's.

Their square block of four cells was the first in a long corridor of them, with thick rock slabs between each block. A shared cylindrical core of plumbing and ventilation occupied the center of the four conjoined cells.

The machine patterns in the rough rock gave mute evidence of having once been mined before becoming prison cell walls.

During designated sleep hours, the mine lowered the embedded lights to five percent, barely enough to avoid obstacles on the way to the fold-down fresher and cold-water faucet.

Just as she was considering yet another few laps around her cell, she heard the soft slaps of Zade's bare feet hitting the metal floor in his cell. She'd heard him nearly as often as she'd gotten up herself.

Impulse born out of need had her rolling out of bed and crossing to his side of her cell. Rather than speak, she reached out with a touch of empath talent.

He vectored straight for her. "You okay?" His soft words were more breath than sound.

"No." The darkness made it easier to admit. "Could you sit with me?" Suddenly she was fifteen again, asking her grandmother to hold her after her brother's murder, hoping the *familiestam* matriarch would bend just this once.

"I'd like that. Be right back."

She sank to the floor in relief and leaned her shoulder against the thick, wide slat. It amused her to imagine that instead of using the fresher, he was quickly hiding myriad griffins who had snuck into his bed after lights out.

When he returned, he sat on his side of the slats. "Would it be alright if we touched?"

In answer, she reached her smaller hand through and brushed cloth with her fingertips. His hand surrounded hers instantly. After hundreds of days of keeping her head down and guard up, it took conscious effort to relax some of her containment. It wouldn't be kind to flood him with her chaotic cauldron of feelings.

He met her halfway.

Just like the first time, their talents twirled toward and around each other like two flames. The raw emotional storm caused by the events in the dining hall had battered them both. She offered him comfort where she could. He soothed her torn and jagged edges.

She couldn't have said how long they sat holding hands, just being together.

A thread of worry snaked through his aura. "Are the cells monitored?"

"No, or half of us would be in the interrogation room by now." Prudence made her add, "But that might change when they get more equipment. Kanogan is a twisted control freak and gets more paranoid by the day."

"Ow!" He jerked, but didn't let go of her hand. "Sorry. Mayek just climbed into my lap. His talons are sharp."

Amusement bubbled in her. "I hope you don't tell him his name means 'Beacon of Light.' His stealthy mates will tease him."

They couldn't prove the griffin was the same one that he and Sutrio had found, but it was a good bet. Stealth griffins weren't common in the cells, even if prisoners offered food stolen right under the watchful prison staff noses.

"Don't listen to her, Mayek," he whispered. "It's a noble name for a clever creature who warned us about the blowout."

"Is Moonlet in there with you, too?" Julke didn't have

the mental connection that Zade and Sutrio had with the griffins, but she found comfort in Moonlet's uncomplicated desire for food and to be the center of attention.

"No, she's hunting, I think." His voice dropped to barely audible. "I know how to get a full land cart. Just need the right moment."

It took her a second to follow the new thought and realize he wasn't talking about transportation. He'd said *landkaart*, an ancient Dutch word for "map." She'd only asked him to get the staff and guards talking about the layout of their living quarters. A complete map of Nova Nine would shorten her timetable considerably.

"If you show me, I'll remember it." That information deserved to be shared. She vowed to find a way to show it to every prisoner with a filer or telepathic talent.

Emotion pulsed, but he contained it. "Can you hide things from nosy telepaths? I don't think Waorani could."

A shudder went through her at the memory of Waorani's agony. "Thank you for worrying, but their telepaths can't read me."

"Really? Me, either. I'm telepath immune." Threads of satisfaction accompanied his declaration. "Torques their jets right off."

A snort of laughter escaped her. "Yes, it does. Even the nicest of them are know-it-alls."

"Probably what killed my last relationship. Alizee wasn't used to having to ask what a lover was thinking, and I wasn't used to answering. Then when the trading company discovered they'd hired a subbin' mindreader, they termed their contract on a flimsy pretext and paid spaceport enforcement for a forced eviction." Threads of sadness and guilt wove through his words. "I don't know why they didn't suspect me."

She caressed the back of his hand with her thumb. "They were blinded by your animal magnetism."

His body vibrated with low laughter, but he held onto her hand. "I got revenge. I was their only hull-repair specialist and resigned at the next stop. Grounded the ship for three weeks while they looked for a replacement. Someone might have flooded the local job net with 'spacer beware' flags about that company. Meanwhile, I looked for a crew that accepted minders. Should have added 'captain isn't a greedy, vengeful asshole' to my selection criteria."

The threads of his regret reminded her of opportunities and deadlines. "Does your greedy former captain have a fast transit ship?" She held her breath for a moment to gather her courage. Breaking the no-trust habit was harder than she'd imagined. "The comms signals that the mine's techs have been chasing are real. I can get a traceable message out without detection. But only once. The techs will jam it when they figure out the content isn't more static."

"Jacker ships have to be fast or they starve. Tell her that Lunaso is sitting on an asteroid-sized haul. She'll round up partners and bend transit to the max to get here and take it from me. I'll give you her ping refs. Ask for a percentage so she doesn't think it's a twist. Warn her about Kanogan's upcoming staffing surge, though. Does your plan call for warning the prisoners this is coming?"

"Actually, it's a fallback plan."

He was silent for a moment. "Okay, I'll bite. What's

the step-forward plan?"

Considering she was hanging onto another empath like he was her deep-space life line, there was no hiding her mix of trepidation and determination.

In her quietest voice, she told him. "Liberate the warden's starship."

Darkness tanked. She needed to see his reaction.

"That sounds highly improbable." He enveloped her hand with both of his. "Sign me up."

She'd forgotten the bone-deep comfort of having someone in her corner. "Your *landkaart* will go a long way toward improving the odds."

"Good." His containment thickened. "Do you have someone waiting for you? Out there? Back home?"

The abrupt subject change took her by surprise. "My *familiestam*, if they've figured out I'm missing. No lovers or claims, if that's what you mean." She hid her sudden nervousness behind her own containment and tried for a nonchalant tone. "What about you?"

"None. Nova Nine blew my plans for a new start. What are claims?"

"Hard to explain. A merger between consenting individuals, perhaps. Historically, our independence and survival depended on claiming things that weren't being appreciated. We're born into or are adopted into *familiestams*, which are about business, property, and governance. Claims are about people who choose to be together and love each other, in whatever ways work for all of them."

"Like a certified group marriage covenant, or a cohab contract?"

She huffed a short breath. "Contracts and covenants are for the *beschaafd*. The cityships were founded by rovers, outcasts, and refugees."

"I'm sensing that 'civilized' isn't a compliment among the Volksstam." His soft chuckle turned into a yawn.

Remorse shot through her. "You need sleep. Sorry I kept you up so long."

"You didn't." His finger stroked the inside of her wrist. "You needed this. I desperately needed this."

"Yes." She let her gratitude loose to cover other, more complex emotions. "But if we don't go to sleep now, there aren't enough stay-awake chems in the galaxy to keep us productive tomorrow. Today. Whenever." She gently restored her containment as she withdrew her hand from his, missing his warmth immediately.

"Come on, Mayek. Bedtime."

The soft griffin trill in response sounded like a sleepy child.

She smiled in the dark. He really had been sleeping with the griffins. Or at least one.

Moving slowly, she listened for the sound of his footfalls and the creak of his bed before sitting on hers. In her head, she composed the content of the communications packet she needed to send. Their best shot at escape was getting out before the warden's anticipated influx of staff and better equipment.

The gods of Chaos did whatever they wanted, of course, but it was fucking cruel of them to make her wait five hundred days in hell to meet someone she could love.

And then make her send the message that would get him killed if her plan failed.

9

NOVA NINE FACILITY • GDAT 3243.121

Zade wouldn't have traded last night's midnight connection with Julke for a fully fluxed interstellar racing yacht, but it was now ten hours into the shift, and his energy reserves were hovering a few degrees above absolute zero.

The only good news was being reunited with Julke, Lantham, and Sutrio when the guards took them to their new work area.

It was his first experience with rhybarium, a key element in flux fuel. Sutrio's cutter sank into the sky-blue deposits like they were pastry in a pan, but she had to be ready to step back when she cut the top of the square she was excavating. Sometimes the sheet of ore separated and shattered the gravity-plate floor.

Like it had a couple of minutes ago. Zade dumped the last shovelful of dull blue crystal into the jig's chute, then stepped back. He'd nominated his noob-self for monitoring the enviro controls and shoveling the shattered ore into Julke's jig. She rolled the machine back so she could transfer the rhybarium into Lantham's collection hopper. The latter looked like it had been rescued from an Abyss trash heap.

Sutrio steadied herself on the mechanized stilts, then lifted the cutter up, making a vertical slice.

Without warning, the whole three-meter excavated face broke apart like an avalanche and spilled onto the gravity plate. It pushed against Sutrio's stilts, knocking her sideways to her left. Her cutter swung wildly and sank deep into the wall. She lost her grip when one of her stilts slipped and sent her to the ground.

Julke's voice got Zade's attention. "Emergency cutoff!" He lunged forward to pull the cable, nearly losing his footing on the new wave of crystalline shards.

Zade helped Sutrio stand as Julke and Lantham climbed off their rigs to survey the situation.

"Well, that's not good," said Lantham. In sign language, he asked Sutrio if she was hurt. She shook her head.

At least, that's what Zade thought the signs meant. Even though the others tried to teach him when they could, he still tanked at it.

The airlock behind them began cycling. *"We're coming in."*

Zade crossed to the scanner to pick it up and power it on, guessing guards would order him to use it on the newly exposed face.

He hid his dismay as Dajoya strode in first, a pugnacious look on her face. She'd been in and out of the work area all morning, micromanaging every task and ordering them to work faster. From her harangues, they'd learned the guards had been chasing more phantom signals the night before and were in line for a bonus if the mine operations met the warden's new production quota.

Lhap Cho followed behind her. He looked as exhausted as Zade felt.

Dajoya halted near the jig and glared. "Sutrio, pull that farkin' cutter out of the goddamn wall. The rest of you slaggers, clean this up and get back to work."

Zade looked at Lhap Cho, willing the guard to remember that protocol called for scanning the newly exposed face for stability. The tunnel didn't have a top plate to protect them or the equipment if the ceiling gave way. Unfortunately, Lhap Cho's frowning attention was on Dajoya.

Zade didn't need a sifter talent to sense that Dajoya was working herself up to violence, like a dreeno addict itching for her next high-glide ride. She might be ramper-fast, but she had tells. Her mech-suited knees flexed and her gloved fingers fidgeted as they hovered near the holster where she kept her stunner. Her rapid, shallow breathing fogged her suit's faceplate. And rage radiated around the black hole of her mental shield like a sun's corona.

He'd learned the hard way that taking a stun meant for her intended target just egged her on. He hated feeling helpless.

Maybe compliance would appease her. He put down the scanner and grabbed the shovel on his way to the mess.

Sutrio checked her stilts, reset the emergency cutoff, then grabbed the cutter's handle and pulled. Where it had been cutting freely before, now it fought her efforts to pull it from the gray rock. Rocking it back and forth and a final, two-handed jerk freed it. She powered down the blade and turned away from the wall.

Something vibrated under his feet. More crystal shards fell, and then a whole section of gray rock wall to the left fell away, leaving a hole big enough for three people to walk through without ducking. Through the swirling clouds of dust, he could see faintly glowing lights and part of a wall of another tunnel.

He froze, watching Julke and the others for a cue on whether to start running.

"Admin," said Lhap Cho, "unexpected tunnel interface in work area Zed-1012-Yang-927. The tunnel looks really old but intact. We'll need map bots and the big scanner. Workgroup 17-C and equipment standing down."

"What?" Dajoya squawked. "It's just a little hole. They can work around it." Her cajoling tone sounded like a sanctioned gravball player trying to work the referee.

Lhap Cho's eyes narrowed. "You go right ahead and ask Operations for a safety procedure variance." His expression morphed into a sarcastic snarl. "We haven't had a blowout in, what, three whole days?"

Dajoya growled and stomped away. Her fingers twitched and her rage corona flared. Her gaze landed on Sutrio. "This is all your fault!"

In an eyeblink, Dajoya's stunner was drawn and Sutrio toppled, falling forward in her stilts and knocking Julke over in a tangle of limbs.

"Two-for-one takedown!" Dajoya's fist pumped triumphantly. She rocked from side to side with a maniacal grin on her face.

Lhap Cho swore a vile oath in Mandarin. "You're warped! This is not a reflex game!"

Lantham stepped in and rolled Sutrio's twitching form off Julke. One of Sutrio's stilts grazed the toe of Dajoya's boot.

She jerked and stunned Lantham in the middle of the big blue circle on the back of his suit. "Three points!"

Lantham collapsed and landed in a boneless heap on top of Sutrio and Julke.

Lhap Cho yanked Dajoya backward and separated her from the stunner with a deft bump and slip. She twisted fast to get away, but Lhap Cho used her momentum to spiral her onto the ground with a hard thump and kneel on her chest.

When she tried to buck him off, he slammed the stunner's business end on her faceplate with a loud crack. "Control yourself *now* or I'll open your helmet and scramble what's left of your maggoty brains."

Long seconds dragged by. Zade held his breath and made a mental note to never, ever to get into a fair fight with the man.

Little by little, the tension drained out of Dajoya's limbs.

Lhap Cho, apparently satisfied with what he saw on the woman's face, stood up and moved back several steps. His eyes and the stunner in his hand tracked her like prey as she climbed to her feet.

When she pointed to her stunner and held out her hand for it, Lhap Cho shook his head. "No." He put the weapon in his suit's big thigh pocket. "You just guaranteed we won't make any quota for the next three days. Didn't you see the mark on Lantham's back?"

"He assaulted me." Dajoya's chin jutted in challenge, as if daring Lhap Cho to say otherwise.

Lhap Cho shook his head, then pointed toward the airlock. "The map bots are here."

With a defiant toss of her head, she spun on her heel and stomped away. She kicked a new dent in the hopper as she passed it on her way out.

Lhap Cho turned to Zade. "Go help the others."

Zade's adrenalin spiked as he dropped the shovel and ran to comply. "Julke?"

"I'm okay." Her voice sounded strong.

Grateful relief flooded him as he wrestled with Lantham's heavy, inert body and rolled him to the side and onto his back. He looked dead, except his exosuit's lifesign indicators were all green.

Sutrio looked more alive, but insensible, as he hastily removed her stilts and rolled her to the other side.

He reached out with a support arm as Julke sat up. A jagged slash across the front of her exosuit alarmed him. He watched her face closely for any sign she was in pain.

As she rolled up to her feet, her empath talent surged to briefly share a chocolatey taste of reassurance.

She waved to get Lhap Cho's attention, then pointed to her chest.

Lhap Cho's lips thinned as he saw the damage. "Dajoya, bring the exosuit repair kit when you come back." He turned away, lips moving in speech that Zade couldn't hear.

Zade had noticed that none of the guards or staff

subvocalized, or even wore earwires. Maybe they all had comms controller implants? As it was, he couldn't fathom how the guards tracked all the various conversations and kept them separated. Prisoners had it easier — they knew the wrong people were *always* listening.

Julke's voice pulled him back from the distraction. "Help me with Lantham."

Together, they dragged the man by his shoulders to the far wall, as much out of the way as possible.

"Will he be okay?" asked Zade.

"Yeah, after a couple of days in an autodoc. He's a sensitive. That's why the medics put the big blue circles on his suit."

Zade cynically suspected the mine only bothered because lost work hours meant lost productivity.

Sutrio was light enough for Zade to carry across his shoulders. Julke helped guide her head as he dropped to one knee and set her down next to Lantham. Sutrio's eyelids fluttered, but she didn't wake.

While his back was still to the guards, he pointed toward the still running big machines, then made what he hoped were the signs to ask if he should turn them off.

Julke shook her head and made the sign for "wait."

He sat next to her, soaking in her deliciously complex and subtle emotional flavors while he watched the progress of the first map bot. It rolled in and halted a meter from the toes of Lhap Cho's boots. Dajoya carried the repair kit bag and stopped behind the bot.

After a few moments of conversation, Lhap Cho threw up his arms in what looked like exasperation and held out his hand. Dajoya gave him the bag. He turned toward Zade and Julke.

"I'm taking Lantham to the medics and bringing back the big scanner." He pointed a thumb behind him. "The other four map bots took a wrong turn. Dajoya's going after them." He let the bag drop to the floor, then used his toe to slide it toward Zade. "Patch Defayensdytr's suit and stay here with Sutrio. One of us will be back soon."

Lhap Cho efficiently strapped a harness around Lantham's torso. Dajoya connected him to Lhap Cho's mech suit like a human-shaped backpack. Neither guard's mental shield leaked emotion, which Zade took as a good sign, especially in Dajoya's case.

Zade counted to thirty after they left and the outer airlock closed, then slid the bag to Julke. "I don't know how to use this kit, but I'll help if you need it."

That was for the benefit of whatever tech was monitoring their comms. He pulled out the purloined tools he'd been collecting in his exosuit's outer pockets ever since he'd discovered that the guards were slacking on nightly suit scans. He pointed toward himself, then pointed the live tech probe toward the map bot.

Julke shook her head vehemently, but her words were casual. "Don't touch the bot, by the way. It'll stun you."

I'm okay, he told her in sign language, then held up his prize, a white triangular card with a security access key. He used the probe's pincers to hold the key near the bot's long side, like he'd seen guards and techs do. The indicators along the oval housing turned from slow-blinking blue to solid orange.

He glanced at his helmet's display to note the time.

Figuring he only had five minutes before someone pinged the bot for status, he scrambled close and rolled it over to expose its tread pods. From there, he found the access points and lifted the bottom base plate to expose the inner mechanism. The first time he'd seen the mine's map bots, he'd recognized them for what they were — repurposed starship hull survey bots. A clever solution, actually. Hull bots were designed to move along an incalloy surface, like the mine's gravity plates were made of, and transmit integrity data to the central shipcomp. The mine's techs added rough-terrain gimbal treads and security, but they were still hull bots.

As such, they required complete reference holomaps to do their job. And he knew where they were stored.

Four minutes left. The enviro unit said the work area's oxygen was too low for comfort and the humidity was low and dropping.

Pocketing the security card, he used the probe to insert a segment of discarded data filament into the blink-and-you'll-miss-it hole in the memory module. Now the harder part.

Three minutes fifteen seconds.

He opened his helmet and unsealed his exosuit's neck yoke. Cold assaulted his naked scalp and exposed ears.

He peeled the front of his suit down to expose the fibre net that handled the onboard comms. The back of his throat felt dry and dusty as he disconnected and pulled off his gloves. Shallow breaths helped control his cough reflex.

One minute fifty seconds.

Carefully, he pried up the bottom of the comms net to

reveal his target, the suit's redundant maintenance records. He forced his icy fingers to press the helpfully well-marked reset control that would flush the memory.

Forty-four seconds.

The fibre filament attached to the bot was too short to reach his suit. Shoving his chest closer, he triggered the sequence that told the bot to upload the data, then hugged the bot tight as a lover so the connection would hold. The hardest part was trusting that it was working. He'd only tested the upload once, with data from a game comp he'd lifted from one of the dining hall staff.

At his self-imposed time limit, he disconnected the filament, sealed up his suit and helmet, put away his tools, and restored the bot's bottom plate. Lastly, he pulled on his gloves and set the bot upright on its treads.

Standing made him lightheaded. His heart still pounding, he drew in three breaths as slowly as he could tolerate. Wheezing gasps might be heard over the comms and bring unwelcome questions.

Turning, he found Julke holding a long strip of tape and grinning at him. He couldn't help but grin back.

She pointed to the bot, then gave the "alert" sign, plus two more he didn't recognize.

Damnit, he wished he'd been more diligent in learning the language. He shook his head.

Sutrio moaned and tried to roll onto her side. "I'm gonna be sick."

Zade hurried over to help Sutrio turn over onto her knees. Julke helped the woman open her helmet just in time. There was little worse in the universe than a closed exosuit full of noxious stink.

After Sutrio's heaving subsided, they helped her seal her helmet and lie down again. Her usually warm brown skin had an ashen undertone that he hoped was just temporary. From what he'd heard from the other prisoners, stunner side-effects varied from minder to minder, but the one common denominator was that it disrupted minder talents for minutes, hours, or even days.

"Workgroup 17-C, report status."

Thank the universe Julke knew what to say to the Admin tech's query. "Sutrio 2043 vomited. She's feeling better now."

Out of the corner of his eye, he saw movement. He turned just in time to see the map bot climbing through the hole leading to the neighboring tunnel. Shit! Had he caused that?

"Workgroup 17-C, why is the map bot moving?"

When Julke looked around, he pointed. At her questioning look, he held up his hands and shook his head. In hull bots, simple data retrieval had nothing to do with active mapping algorithms.

"No idea." She climbed to her feet. "It just took off. Looks like it's headed for the old tunnel."

"Workgroup 17-C, prevent the bot from leaving."

"How?" Julke's voice held a touch of asperity. "We can't touch it."

The bot's work light went dark just as it vanished into the darkness.

"Workgroup 17-C. Defenses disabled. We can't afford to lose any more bots. Retrieve it now." The midrange voice had a tinge of panic.

"On our way." She took a step toward the hole, then

hesitated. "Lunaso, turn the jig to face the hole so we have more light."

He did as she asked. He detoured to pull two hand lights and a tension-reel of thin cable from the jig's maintenance toolbox and went after her. Fear made him hurry. He hoped that overconfidence in his scheme hadn't put them all in danger.

10

Julke cautiously stepped through the breach and onto the plate, testing it with her foot before committing the rest of her. In the really old plates, sometimes the built-in gravity generators failed in spots, making it feel like walking on a sponge. The floor lights glowed too faintly to see where the bot went.

Under any other circumstances, she'd wait right there for a few minutes, then tell Admin the bot had vanished. But Zade's spikes of alarm made her worry that he still needed that bot to get the map. At least an old tunnel was better than being in the Abyss.

He came up behind her and showed her a cable reel, then gave her a light. She should have thought of both. Good thing she had a smart man on her side who did.

They wedged the reel housing under a heavy rock, then ran the line through her suit's waist straps and tied the end tightly to his.

He pointed his light toward the ceiling. It was higher

than usual, and made of eroded sponge rock, like the ceiling in the refinery.

She swept her light in a slow arc on the floor. No map bot. No dust for it to leave tracks in, either. Dust danced in the air, blowing right to left. Odd, because she'd have expected it to be blowing in from the work area behind them. "The bot can't have gone far."

He waved his light to get her attention, then circled his finger upward and gave her the sign for griffins.

She wished she could ask him what kind, which would give her a clue about the nearby environment. But the sooner they got out, the better. "You go left, I'll go right. We'll cover twice as much ground." The improvised safety line still would let them find their way back to each other and the anchor.

He turned and walked away. Her suit vibrated as the cable slid through her waist straps.

She walked to the right as fast as she dared. The guards usually complained about how slow the map bots moved, but maybe this one liked speed. CGC machines didn't have unique personalities like Volkszang tech did, but complex algorithms could make it seem that way. Couldn't be an AI, or the warden would have had it flatlined. Prison rumors said he was afraid of them.

Ahead, the tunnel curved sharply down and left. She stopped at the top of the turn and directed her light forward. Movement caught her eye.

The little bot was valiantly climbing a tall pile of rubble that looked like another tunnel wall failure. "Zade, I found the bot. Come help me catch it."

"On my way."

She walked fast toward the rubble pile because the determined bot was already at the top and about to disappear from view. Zade, with his longer legs, caught up with her quickly, then passed her.

When she got in front of the rubble, she stopped in her tracks. Clearly visible through the hole in the tunnel wall was a door. And not just any door, but a starship's five-meter antique exterior loading-bay airlock door, complete with original markings.

Zade was already scrambling over the low edge of the rubble pile, intent on following his prey. She could tell when he finally noticed the door because he stopped short just like she had.

Following his path, she stepped over the rubble and through the opening. To her right, the tunnel dead-ended. The left side curved sharply into darkness.

The bot ran into the door and bounced back. The airlock's door frame lit up, and the control panel bezel began a steady blink, but the iris leaves of the door itself stayed closed.

Zade scooped up the bot and tucked into his arm and against his chest, its gimbal treads facing out. He pulled his front exosuit strap around its flat bottom to help secure it. The treads stopped wiggling after a bit.

The bot had probably expected the door to open for it like all mine airlocks did. She eyed the blinking control panel again. The security office changed the universal emergency access code so often that the staff had taken to writing the new one down in places they thought were secret.

Priorities pulled at her. They'd gotten what they came

for, but now she was reluctant to leave. A crazy idea formed in her mind.

He pointed toward the door, then made the sign for griffins.

"This tunnel" — he said, shining his light on the door's intricate filigree decoration— "looks old enough to have been made by the Central League Armed Forces."

"Workgroup 17-C. The bot has stopped moving. Do you have it?"

"Close," Julke replied. The Admin tech's peevish tone meant they'd run out of patience soon, but instinct was pushing her. "Let's try this."

She took off her left glove and put her palm on the flat control panel. Cold seeped into her fingers and joints. Just as she was about to give up, the full display finally woke up. Mandarin words invited her to supply the code. She entered the oldest universal one from her inherited memories, then hurriedly pulled her glove back on and sealed it. Her whole arm ached.

The bezel turned solid dark red.

Zade stepped closer to look at the panel.

The bezel flashed blue for a moment, then alternated between blue and red, like it couldn't make up its mind.

Inspired, she pulled him and the bot closer to the threshold. The bezel stayed blue. The airlock's door irised open.

A forceful intake of wind pulled both her and Zade forward a couple of steps before she caught her balance. Lights blazed on, revealing a gridded platform surrounded by loose mesh walls. It took her a moment to realize it was a lift cage, and she'd seen it before in her memories.

ZADE WATCHED Julke closely for what she wanted to do. Not being able to talk freely seriously torqued his jets.

His curiosity was in overdrive, but he also liked living. And he felt obligated to get the stolen holomaps to the other prisoners. She knew Nova Nine far better than he did, and carrying the bot hindered his ability to run or handle trouble.

"Workgroup 17-C. Did you damage the map bot? It's offline."

"No," answered Julke. "It's gone behind an old rockfall with xeronium tracings. We're trying to get it out." She waved him forward, then signed to stop after he'd only taken two steps. "I'll go around."

"Workgroup 17-C, where are you? Your comms are breaking up."

Julke stepped around him and back into the tunnel to the rubble. She wrestled a large rock free. "We're in the tunnel where you told us to go. I don't see any identifiers." She half-rolled, half-dragged the rock to rest on the threshold of the open airlock.

"Workgroup 17-C. If you can't get the bot within five minutes, return to the assigned work area without it."

"Okay." She stepped closer to him and drew his attention to her oxy readout, which showed the air quality was now in acceptable range. When she opened her helmet, he did the same. Cold air smacked him in the face, but he didn't care.

"Five minutes, then we go back." She spoke soft and fast. "This is a lift. Nova Nine's ship hangar has one just like it. I think this lift, or maybe whatever this space is, blocks the mine's comms and trackers." She pointed to what looked like the lift's control. "Instincts are pushing me hard to go up one level and take a look. I can't tell you why, or what we'll find. Just that it's important."

He knew the feeling. Moreover, he trusted her. "Then let's look." He touched the cable between them. "I know I'm not usually the voice of caution, but this is our only way back out if we get lost. Can we make the airlock stay open while we're exploring?"

"No time to experiment. The rock should keep the door from closing. I think your bot's universal codes helped make it open in the first place."

Her intensity sparked his sense of adventure. He hitched the bot up higher on his hip. "Then I'm green go."

She did something at the control panel. As the lift rose quickly and smoothly. he watched to make sure the cable came with them. It had plenty of length, but it wasn't the tough monofibre line they'd had when exploring the Abyss.

When the lift cage stopped, she touched another control. The back wall of the cage lifted like a gate, revealing a narrow metal platform with a gold-encrusted filigree railing.

The second she stepped onto the platform, lights blazed on. A mellifluous synth voice welcomed her in Mandarin as High Lord Warden Nimasang Jinzuh, invited her to behold the glory of her unparalleled collection, and asked which chariot she would like to fly this auspicious day.

More lights blinked on.

And on, and on, and on...

The best hallucinogens in the galaxy could have never given him a vision like this. A huge cavern, bigger than the refinery, filled with starships. Antique personal starships.

They were stored in a giant metal frame. He lost count at thirty, and he couldn't see how far down the cavern went, or how many were on the other side. Each ship rested on its own sliding platform and had cables and lines attached. The unknown collector favored retro-advanced design and big engines.

And flying among them, griffins. All four breeds, from what he could see, though mostly common and stealth. They seemed to be treating the levels like a giant vertical habitat built just for griffins. The bright lights had obviously disturbed them. He sensed echoes of their distress.

"If Lantham could see this, he'd think he'd transited to the paradise dimension." He laughed. "Sutrio, too. Now we know why the staff will never be able to keep griffins out of the mine."

"The comms satellite is really close." She looked up, then whistled. "Holy gods of... You could launch everything at once through those airlocks. Only cityships have anything like these."

Two monstrously big airlocks spanned the entire cavern ceiling. He wondered where they opened. Near the rest of the facility? And how long did they take to open?

Speaking of time, how long had they been gawking at the wonder of the ages? He pulled on the cable to get Julke's attention. "Five minutes."

"Shit." Reluctance etched her face, but she turned

away and stepped with him into the lift. She closed the lift gate and used the controls to send the lift down.

Questions crowded into his mind. "Do you think Kanogan knows about this?"

She shook her head. "I doubt anyone alive does. And he'd never let stinking griffins stay. He collects people, not things." She paused, then caught his gaze. "I'm re-thinking my original step-forward plan."

The gleam in her eye gave him an inkling of where she was headed. He nodded gravely. "You're right. Not bold enough."

"Anyone can make off with a single starship." She gave him an invitingly evil grin. "But how many can say they've liberated an entire warden's fleet?"

He grinned back. "Go big *and* go home."

The lift stopped at the level where their cable snaked out the airlock doorway.

Just as he was about to reseal his helmet, she stepped close. "I know this isn't the best timing, but could I interest you in a kiss? I've made a recent vow not to let golden opportunities slip by again."

"Yes, please." He opened his right arm to hold her as she raised on her toes. The exosuits made it awkward, but he didn't care. The touch of her lips and the scent of her breath imprinted him like he was a newly hatched griffin.

Even though she'd contained her emotions, he felt her reluctance as she pulled away and sealed her helmet.

He felt all that and more as he sealed his own. He made his own vow to do everything in his power to keep this brilliant, nova-sexy woman in his life.

In the privacy of his luxurious fresher, Drow Kanogan slipped naked into the almost too-hot waters of his bath to drift, letting the undulating currents soothe his aching hips. No denying that the pain was getting worse with each passing day. The gently frothing water hid the worst of the disfigurement, just like the distortion hood and robe saved him from seeing his reflection in the eyes of others.

He missed the comforts and pleasures of civilization. He missed being beautiful. His ruined body could be fixed on any of a hundred planets in the CGC, but that had to wait another year until he'd built up the resources to ensure his absolute safety. Until then, he'd have to limp along with massages, baths, and pain patches.

Lately, his operation had suffered from mistakes by others, but things were already improving. Working the prisoners longer hours gave him extra product to sell, and more profits to invest in improving capacity. By his calculations, the coming influx of people and equipment would pay for itself in two hundred days.

And if rumors were true about trouble coming in the galaxy, he could name his price for the precious commodities that Nova Nine produced. Unrest offered plenty of opportunities for smart entrepreneurs with experience in building empires to acquire–

The door irised open to admit Loulez, one of his protectors. She stood stiffly, eyes focused on the wall. "Your pardon, sir. Security Chief Taiyang must speak with you immediately."

He frowned as he pulled himself back to the steps. "This had better not be another blowout." She knew better than to interrupt his therapy if it wasn't serious.

"No, sir. Visitors."

Despite the steamy heat as he climbed out of the water, his stomach turned cold. "Robe."

She vanished as he was limping to the solardry. In moments, she returned with both his robe and hood as he stepped into the exoframe and connected it to his obstinate cybernetic leg. He slid his flesh-and-blood foot into the adaptive boot built into the frame, then sealed his robe.

In his office, built by previous wardens to impress, he pulled on his hood, then pinged Taiyang. She answered immediately. From the holo image's background, she was in the weapons control center.

"I'll assume you've confirmed our visitors aren't an early delivery of our new supplies, and that our pharma partners know nothing about them."

"Yes, sir. Three ships dropped out of transit seventeen

minutes ago. Ship configuration is typical jacker. No identifiers, no comms, extra armor and weapons ports. We're assembling the visuals now."

Kanogan had known this day would come. Even with the vastly improved security measures he'd implemented, secrets were hard to keep forever. Growing a nearly forgotten black hole of a political punishment prison into a major mining operation using pharma money had inherent risks. He'd spent most of the first year's pharma rent on improving defenses.

"Wake the *Songbird*. Let's see if they go for it. And activate the transit point's swarm."

Taiyang touched a display with deft fingers. "Done."

When he'd first arrived at Nova Nine, more than half the loading ship hangar had been occupied by a badly damaged warship from the Central League Armed Forces, complete with typical over-the-top design and an absurdly long name. Once he'd seen Nova Nine's potential and promoted himself to warden via a few carefully timed disappearances, he'd ordered the ship towed to a spot near the transit jump point to act as a honeypot.

Taiyang sat up straighter. "Incoming message." She touched a control.

"To whom it may concern," a synth voice stated in Standard English. *"We intercepted an equipment shipment addressed to Nova Nine. We are looking for someone and would like to negotiate a trade."* The message repeated in Mandarin. A brief holovid of several pallets of mine excavation machines accompanied the audio.

Taiyang's face hardened. "I recommend destroying the intruders immediately. They already know too much."

"No, not yet. They might have more ships on the way. The swarm isn't big enough to handle multiple waves of attackers." Besides, losing the equipment the jackers carried would set his timetable back at least half a year. His hip couldn't wait that long.

He needed more information. "Bounce a reply via the *Songbird*. Ask them who they're looking for."

Taiyang's expression went blank. "Respectfully, sir, they're very likely guessing. We'll be giving up the advantage of silence."

That was the trouble with security people. Always risk-averse, and thinking they knew better than he did how to handle miscreants. "Send the message, Ms. Taiyang."

The prompt answer was unexpected.

He stood. "Send the prisoners to lockdown immediately and ready our defenses. Get all the data you can on the intruders. And get the Interrogation Team to find out what makes that man so valuable."

12

Julke sat in the cab of the collection hopper and watched as Zade's jig slowly emptied its contents into the chute. One more load and she'd run the compactor.

Exhaustion was slowing her down, but the press of time kept her going. So did the nutrient-rich stay-awake chems the mine's medics handed out like after-dinner sweets. After all, awake workers were productive workers.

It had been four days since the life-altering discovery of the cavern of ships. She'd spent every non-work hour thereafter pulling together every resource and alliance she had to organize the prisoners into a run for the cavern of ships.

She regretted allowing the network she'd been knitting since her arrival at Nova Nine to fray. Despair and loneliness were poor excuses, but they were all she had. The big blowout a few ten-days ago had cost them prisoners with needed talents and knowledge. She couldn't change the past, so they'd have to work around it.

Zade's map was one of three critical keys. He'd not only successfully copied it, but figured out how to upload it to prisoner exosuit memory. Now their heads-up helmet display could show the whole map with the press of a control. It wasn't perfect — zooming in and out on a given section took practice, and three-dimensional orientation on a two-dimensional display was confusing — but it gave them a fighting chance. She'd memorized it, and asked all the other filers to do so, too, but not everyone could follow a navigator's map.

The second key was Lantham, who'd returned to the workgroup two days ago after his autodoc healing session. The gods of Chaos had been in a merciful mood. Their workgroup was still assigned to the rhybarium seam. The tunnel breach had only been sealed with a tacked tarp. The guards were increasingly absent, sent to chase multiple phantom comms signals and misbehaving map bots.

Consequently, with Zade and Sutrio working their asses off to maintain productivity, she'd been able to sneak Lantham into the cavern to see for himself. After his second, solo foray later that afternoon, he'd provided a list of the best ships to choose, and said the giant scaffold with ship platforms was a standard military configuration for its time. Based on the lines and cables connected to each ship, he believed the scaffold's automated systems were powered by a stockpile of refined xeronium that kept the ships launch-ready. He also took on the task of making sure each ship got a pilot and a navigator. The assignments would undoubtedly change once they got their hands on the actual ships.

Prughal, the enviro systems specialist, said no enviro

system of the era could have kept breathable air in the huge cavern for two hundred years. In their opinion, the ships themselves were supplying the oxygen, humidity, and temperature regulation. Doing so would have both saved money and kept the complex ship systems in running order. Julke had a plan to sneak Prughal into the cavern for a hands-on evaluation later that shift. It would take good timing and better luck, but these days, what didn't?

No one felt confident that the ships had flux fuel for their transit drives. It would be a problem in the long run, but fully powered system engines would get them off Nova Nine and in a position to be rescued. Assuming her messages reached the right people.

The third key was opening the giant overhead airlocks. She was still working on that one.

Timing was also critical. While the cavern had thin but breathable air, the tunnels to it likely didn't. The prisoners would need exosuits to get to the cavern. Therefore, the escape would have to be early in a work shift, when oxygen and water were fully charged.

And they weren't going without as many griffins as they could carry. Sutrio nominated herself as the queen of the griffins. She'd have help from Zade in calling the griffins to them. Whether they'd go into the ships and stay there for the launch was another matter.

At the newly exposed rock face, nine meters beyond the tunnel tarp, Lantham checked the strap of his stilt, then picked up the cutter.

"Workgroup 17-C. Shift over. Stop operations. Secure equipment. Stand by for escort to the cells. Acknowledge and report individually."

Lantham hesitated, then turned off the cutter and announced that he'd done so. She, Sutrio, and Zade all followed suit, then lined up next to the enviro unit. The instructions were the same as always. The timing most definitely was not. The mine hadn't ever ended a shift after only one hour.

Lhap Cho and Dajoya entered through the airlock. Their expressions were forbidding and their shields tight as they ushered them into the access tunnel for the long walk to the mine exit.

Except they didn't go to the decontamination transition zone, they marched straight to the seldom-used emergency door that took them straight to the cells. A quick glance down the hall proved they weren't the only prisoners being ordered into their block, still wearing their exosuits, locked in their cells, and told to lie down and shut up.

All except Zade.

Julke fought to keep all expression off her face as Dajoya took him aside, slapped shackles on his wrists. She clearly enjoyed announcing that he had an appointment with the interrogation team.

ZADE THOUGHT he knew what terror was, but each step closer to the interrogation rooms proved he'd been wrong.

The enforcer who took custody of him shoved him through an entrance and shut the door.

The bright room had one knee-high medical corpse

cart and two red-sashed women, both holding amped-up shocksticks.

The taller woman unlocked his shackles, then pointed her shockstick toward him. "Take off your exosuit and lie down."

He complied without argument, remembering what the shockstick could do.

When the woman tapped a control, the cart wrapped his ankles and upper body in metal bands. He was getting tired of lying on carts naked.

A familiar pressure built in his head, more painful than he'd ever felt, then subsided.

"Fuck." The short, muscular woman made a face. "He really is telepath immune. We'll have to do this the hard way." When she stepped aside, he saw a medic's tray of jets. His stomach bottomed out as she selected one and primed it.

The tall woman leaned over him. "What was your last job before Shenyan Surkai Space Station?"

"Trade expediter." Jacker slang for sellers of stolen goods to buyers who paid in anonymous cashflow chips and didn't ask questions.

Annoyance crossed her face. "What ship?"

"Ebion Alba." That was the name he'd put on his quals list. It came to him, belatedly, that a sifter was probably nearby and calibrating his honesty.

The short woman stepped closer and knelt, drug jet in her hand. "We don't have time for Yes-and-No. The Warden wants answers now."

He let his alarm show on his face. "Er, did you check my record? I'm allergic to a lot of chems. The intake medics nearly killed me. Not that I *want* to be interrogated, but better that than dead."

The short woman hesitated, then swore. "Truth." She rose to her feet, crossed to the tray, and picked up a tablet.

The tall woman rested her fists on her hips. "Let's cut to the core. Why would three jacker ships show up on our very well-hidden doorstep looking for one man?"

Zade blinked. He didn't believe in coincidence. They could only be the highly motivated Fazhian and her allies.

The fallback distraction he'd promised Julke had come early. He hoped to the stars she was taking advantage of it. He'd have to do his part for as long as he could. "What man?"

The tall woman gave him a silent, considering look. "What do you know about Riorojo Waorani?"

"Huh?" He didn't have to pretend confusion. "Nothing." Remembering the nearby sifter listening for lies, he added, "Well, I know he's a... he *was* a sifter and a teke. I guess he's a Red Team guardian now? I don't know how long that takes."

The short woman came back with a different jet and slammed it into his hip. "Let's try this again."

This was going to be a long farking' day. He couldn't guess what Fazhian's game was, but he was willing to play along if it kept the interrogation team away from Julke.

He didn't want to die for her. He wanted to live for her and follow her across the galaxy and find out what claiming meant. But if he couldn't do any of those things, he could give her and the prisoners what they need most: time.

13

NOVA NINE FACILITY • GDAT 3243.125

J ulke prayed to every god she knew that the prisoners were doing like she told them and going straight for the cavern of ships. Not detouring like she was.

Immediately after locking the cells, the mine guards had vanished. Fifteen minutes later, three mercenaries who belonged to the pharma company had shown up to keep an eye on them.

Someone forgot to remind the mercenaries they'd be watching pissed off prisoners who had multiple minder talents and practice working together to extract information from the unwary.

Not only did they learn about the three jacker ships, but they now knew some of Nova Nine's defenses. Not to mention the access codes for the pharma's private weapons storage locker, ship hangar, and the two corporate starships therein.

All the prisoners recognized a gift from the gods when they saw it, but they couldn't agree on when to take it. She'd finally realized they were waiting for her.

So she gave the order.

Little Moonlet went with Sutrio, but Mayek wrapped himself around Julke's forearm like a vambrace and refused to budge. Within seconds, he looked like an extra bit of armor on her suit.

Once the prisoners used the stolen codes to get out of their cells and subdue the guards, she'd led the vanguard toward the emergency exits that would take them to the tunnels. Then she'd used her *negerensgave* talent to make them look elsewhere long enough to slip away.

The maps in her head gave her the shortest route to the interrogation area, where two rooms were clearly marked. The presence of the negligently slouching enforcer told her which room to try first. With judicious use of her talents, the enforcer was soon slumped on the floor, and she was now armed.

Her aura talent told her three people — including Zade's unique pattern — were in the room in front of her. A fourth seemed farther away, perhaps in the other room. No time for subtlety.

She banged on the door with the butt of her newly acquired shock baton. "Sirs? Hate to interrupt, but you need to see this."

As she'd hoped, her peremptory tone sparked irritation in two of the room's occupants. She used her empath talent to nudge it up into anger. CGC-trained telepaths like those on the warden's interrogation team often discounted empathy as beneath their notice, so they forgot to shield against it.

The hinged door slammed open. The woman didn't have a chance to speak before Julke stunned her, then the shorter woman near a medic tray. She shot each of them a second time just to be sure. And when the third telepath came charging into the room, she shot him twice, too.

Only then could she afford to look at Zade to see what damage they'd done to him.

He looked back at her with a clear-eyed gaze and emotions flowing freely, dancing with hers. "Is this a good time to tell you I love you?"

She hadn't cried in five hundred days of captivity, but tears threatened now. "The best possible time."

Freeing him and getting him into his exosuit took more time than she'd hoped. "You brought Mayek!" His hands shook badly as he tried to pet the griffin. "Have I told you I love you?"

She frowned at the two deep bruises forming on his hip. "What did they juice you with?"

"No clue. Made me cold and twitchy." He pulled on his gloves. Mayek transferred himself from Julke's arm to Zade's.

Julke glanced at the clock display. "Can you run?"

He gave her a wink. "Let's find out."

Their assigned route through the tunnels put them at the bottom of the cavern. Zade was able to run, but the abrupt gravity direction changes disoriented him.

After the second time running into a wall, Mayek launched and flew ahead. Instead of leaving them, however, the griffin flew back and forth, capturing Zade's attention and guiding him like he was a griffin baby taking his first flight.

Julke projected all the gratitude she could to the griffin. Following the map and watching out for trouble took all her concentration. They'd have been twice as slow without Mayek's help.

At last, they reached the cavern floor where the lift gates awaited. She checked her oximeter then told Zade he could unseal. Mayek settled on Zade's shoulders. Opening her helmet again felt good.

Word of their arrival spread on the wings of thought.

A lanky Volksstam prisoner named Visser met them at the lift. "Our people are in D-71. Lunaso is A-40."

"Nope." She grabbed Zade's upper arm possessively. "They gave him to me. I'm keeping him."

Visser blinked, then shrugged.

Zade turned to her with a solemn look. "Did you just claim me?"

Before she could answer, a call went out over the telepathic net that Sutrio needed Zade's help with the griffins. Julke relayed the message and told him how to find her.

Turning to Visser, she asked about the overhead airlocks problem.

"Solved. But we'll be fish in a barrel for the ten minutes it takes them to open."

She gave him a tired smile. "I have an idea for that. Let me talk to Lantham."

ZADE MET Sutrio on the collector's viewing platform at the top of the cavern. The woman had bruises like saucers under her eyes, but she'd explained it was just blowback from talent overuse. "I've called all the griffins I can and gotten them into ships, but the rock griffins in the Abyss won't listen. They might come for you." A corner of her mouth twitched in a smile. "And Mayek."

"Where is the Abyss from here?"

She pointed down. "Below the bottom gravity plates. We discovered a ship-sized breach in the far corner. Probably explains the variable winds and the oxygen in the Abyss."

"Okay, I'll try. I feel like I should tell you I'm high-gliding on mystery chems from the interrogation team. Once those burn out, I might collapse."

"Fair enough. Sit down now, then. You're too heavy for me to catch. What's your blowback?"

"Migraine headache." He did as she asked.

"Fun." She waved an expansive hand. "They're all yours."

He activated his talent a bit, just to get a sense of the griffins already nearby. Mayek felt like a warm glow in his mind.

Closing his eyes, he visualized the Abyss and the hole that led to the cavern. He took a slow, deep breath, then let his talent loose.

Come with me, he beckoned them. *We're all going to a new home.* The words were just sounds to carry his emotions and images. He included the love he felt for Mayek.

The rock griffins responded immediately, like they'd been longing to hear from him. He couldn't tell how many. He continued beckoning until Sutrio put a hand on his shoulder. "That's done it. Tell them you like me, and I'll get them sorted."

He pictured Sutrio, and how clever she was and how much he and Mayek trusted her, then let the connection go. Exhaustion was winning the war against the chems. And a migraine was lurking in the shadows.

Sounds of a commotion below galvanized him. The rock griffins were suddenly scared and mad. They needed his help.

JULKE WIPED sweat off her neck and hid in the shadow of a scaffold cross-brace, waiting for her next ambush victim. Her stolen beamer had plenty of charge, but she had no armor if anyone shot back.

The escapees had been unbelievably lucky up until five minutes ago. Then trouble came swarming out of the tunnels, and the fight was on.

The enforcers and the pharma mercenaries were bad enough, but they'd never seen the caverns and their orders seem to only allow disabling the prisoners. The prisoners' counterpunch pushed a large portion of the attackers back out in the tunnels and stranded them there.

But the relentless mech-suited warden's guardians went straight for the kill. Avoiding them worked for a while, but they were unstoppable.

Until the rock griffin began vomiting on guardian helmets. The noxious mass melted through the faceplate and burned whatever delicate tech and tender flesh it found.

Warden's guardians didn't scream, they just slowed, faltered, and died. She knew they were probably already brain dead the moment they were fitted into their red armor, but it was still hard to watch their deaths. Thank the gods that she hadn't recognized any of them as former prisoners. That would have been a memory she could do without.

The prisoners' telepathic net was stretched to the breaking point when the news came that the griffins were in. Time to seal up the ships and get ready to launch.

Zade met her at their ship's platform, and together they stumbled through the airlock. Mayek warbled a greeting to her.

Once inside the ship, which was small but sleek, she wasn't the least bit surprised to see the loading area held at least a dozen rock griffins, and a few more representatives of the other three breeds. They followed Zade like a lodestar. The smaller hold where Visser directed them soon looked like an animal rehab center for griffins.

Visser pointed toward some jump seats and told them to strap in. He muttered something about wobbly ships as he left them alone with the griffins.

Their seats were about a meter apart. Keeping in mind the ship was at least one hundred fifty years old, she tested hers first before committing her full weight. "Was it your idea or Sutrio's to get the rock griffins to attack?"

"The griffins, actually, but they kept bouncing off armor. Sutrio remembered their stomach contents are extremely caustic. Sutrio directed them to the guardians. I convinced them it was a good idea."

She smiled and touched two fingers to her heart. "Please thank the griffins for me."

"I hate to ask, but..." Zade hooked a web across his lap.

"Where are the mine guards? Where are the rest of Kanogan's guardians? What about the mercs? This feels too... easy."

"I think lucky feels like easy, sometimes." She hooked her own web tight and let her short legs swing. "The mine guards are operating the weapons platforms. Kanogan will keep some guardians for himself. We don't know about the mercs, but they only signed on to protect the labs. And only the gods know what the mine staff or the pharma researchers are doing, but we think they're non-combatants." She closed her eyes for a long sigh. "We're not out of the dust swarm yet."

One of the ghost-colored rock griffins sidled over to Zade and curled its tail around his boot. The griffin hissed in obvious contentment and rested its beak on its forelegs. Two others sidled closer, too.

"What about the fish-in-a-barrel problem?" He frowned. "Or the fish jumping out of the barrel problem, for that matter?"

She kept forgetting that his immunity meant he couldn't have learned all their plans from the prisoners' telepathic connection. "We have a couple of illusionists in our network. We'll all amplify them for the next ten minutes until the airlocks open." Her eyes felt gritty and her mouth tasted metallic. "After that, we'll use chaos patterns to fly as far and fast as we can. We hope with twenty ships, the guns won't know where to shoot."

"I don't know if it's important, but if you believe the interrogators, the jackers asked for Waorani, not me. They interrogated me because I was recruited in the same bunch. They thought I might be his partner and know what made him so valuable." He frowned. "Captain Fazhian doesn't usually triangulate like that. She's a berserker when she's mad, and an ambush stalker when she's not."

Julke shook her head. "I don't know what it means, but I'll tell the net." It took just a moment to reconnect and share Zade's information. Her energy reserves were nearly gone. "I tank at military strategy. My gift is getting people to work together. Now we have to trust the pilots and navigators and engineers to get us out of here and keep us alive until our rescuers arrive."

And she still had to pass on key information to her people. Then she wanted to sleep for ten days, then get lost somewhere for a while with just Zade and maybe a griffin or two to keep them company. She hoped bold little Moonlet had made it into one of the ships.

The airlock clanked and beeped as it finished closing. The pilot announced that it was six minutes until launch. Though she shied away from the thought, she knew they'd lose some ships. Stress and exhaustion jangled her nerves. Right now, all she wanted was to climb into Zade's lap like little Mayek already had.

He must have felt her distress, because his empathy talent wrapped hers in warmth and sympathy. "So, since we have time to kill, tell me more about this Volksstam claiming thing. What if the claimer is a princess among her people, and the claimee is a *beschaafd* noob? An orphan who spent all his savings on a down payment for a frontier planet homestead, but will lose it when he doesn't show up within the next two standard days to register the claim?"

That startled her. "Do you want to live on a planet? They have an awful lot of... weather."

A smile creased his face. "We have this new invention called buildings. Perhaps you've heard of them? But never mind. Meeting a pirate princess has given me other ideas." His emotional containment dropped, hiding nothing. "I meant it when I said I love you. I'd like to stay with you, but not if it puts you at odds with your people. I haven't forgotten that you have information they need. If they'll listen better without me as a distraction..."

"They'll either listen or they won't." His honesty humbled her. She let her emotions dance with his and showed him everything in her heart. "I love you, Zade Lunaso. I want to stay with you. And just so you know, you are sexy as hell. I want to do more than just hold hands. It involves lots of skin on skin."

"I can't begin to tell you the hot dreams I had about you." He gave her a saucy grin. "But I'd like to show you."

"Launch in two minutes."

The announcement brought her back to reality. Nearly a hundred lives depended on surprise, boldness, and luck. And it was all out of her hands now.

She hoped the gods of Chaos were in a generous mood.

14

Z ade clamped down hard on his containment as the airlock opened. He didn't want to stress Julke with his nervous anticipation. She had enough to deal with.

The Volksstam starship *Ars Memoriae* that was about to receive them belonged to Julke's grandmother and *familiestam* matriarch, Benthe Robynsdytr. She'd brought staff and trusted allies with her. Not to mention nine other Volksstam ships.

In spare moments, he'd been poring over the holos of them, since he'd only ever seen one from a distance. He bet Lantham, who had thankfully made it out alive, had been doing the same.

Julke's plea for aid had also drawn a small fleet of indie traders, and even a few ships from the frontier worlds in her former trading network. The group of thirty-six ships was far more than she or anyone else had anticipated.

The three days between the desperate launch and the arrival of the rescuers had been a pendulum of terror and boredom. Their shipmates declared the ship to be spaceworthy, but not trustworthy enough for anyone to remove their exosuits. They only had one flavor of mealpacks that the prisoners had been hoarding for the escape.

No flux fuel meant they weren't going far, but that was just as well, since none of the crew wanted to take a chance on the ship's wildly out-of-date navigation data. The system engine was more than enough to get them out of weapons range in a hurry.

Unfortunately, six of the twenty launched ships hadn't been so lucky. And worse, they only knew what had happened to two of them. The other four had simply vanished. Once the rest of the scattered ships had established tight-beam comms, they'd held a moment of silence to mourn the friends they had lost.

After they'd gone far enough, the pilot let *Wobbly*, their newly christened ship, drift on its own. With no onboard weapons, not even debris lasers, their only defense was pretending to be one with the lifeless void.

Julke slept like the dead. Without stay-awake chems, her body had cratered. He'd carried her to the narrow bed in one of the quaint little staterooms and attached a strap to her suit in case they lost gravity. She only woke to down the water pouches he left for her.

He slept nearby on the floor on a makeshift mattress of blankets. Just as well, because Mayek and other griffins kept wanting to snuggle with him, and their claws tore up the bedding. Three of the rock griffins in particular had apparently adopted him. They orbited him wherever he went, so it amused him to name them after old Earth system planets.

The other seventeen griffins explored everywhere and tried to eat anything, to the exasperation of the rest of the crew. He didn't have Sutrio's enviable gift of mentally connecting to griffin thoughts, but he could project disappointment and warning when their behavior got out of hand. At least he figured out how to train the griffins to poop in designated areas, or the crew would have probably locked them all in the hold.

When he wasn't fishing pieces of mealpack trays out of impromptu griffin nests, he and Lantham provided operations advice to other surviving ships with crews who didn't have as much experience. All the ships turned out to have the same innovative hydroponics-enviro system design that was better than some modern ships. Lantham and Prughal, the enviro specialist, spent long hours examining them.

Then Julke's help arrived. He'd needed to wake her for proof of life, and so she could handle the sometimes confusing and sometimes fraught negotiations. Indie traders, frontier planet defenders, and Volksstam ship leaders were understandably wary of one another.

Prisoners needed to be returned to their families and former lives. A few needed new lives. They all needed medical and stress-trauma care.

Not to mention, the hundred-plus griffins packed into the antique ships all needed new homes as well.

Julke sat in on all the meetings, using her presence and her words to remind them why they were all there. He sat in so he could learn, and support Julke if she needed it.

Nova Nine had ceased all communications. An impenetrable barrage of defenses shot at anything that got too close. None of the rescue ships were inclined to dig Kanogan or the pharma company minions out of their rat's nest. It was theorized they'd already escaped and left a weapons AI to defend the asteroid. Zade wasn't so sure, considering how much the warden disliked AIs.

It didn't matter. Nova Nine would never be a prisoner trap again. Too many people now knew where it was and what it had. It was only a matter of time before the hyenas arrived to take it apart.

Also, something, maybe opening the airlocks or launching so many ships, had unblocked the emergency comms satellite. It had been broadcasting away ever since. That would eventually draw the CGC military to investigate why a nearly two-hundred-year-old comms node was now suddenly back online.

The jackers who were after Waorani turned out to be a rival pharma company's mercenaries masquerading as jackers. Kanogan's pharma company partner had been lax about security. The rival firm knew just enough to track the shipment of recruits, so they'd sent Waorani. When he disappeared, they hijacked a cargo as a bargaining chip and came looking. They'd just about decided to leave when the Volksstam fleet arrived and detained them for questioning.

Then Julke's grandmother had invited her and the other four Volksstam to her personal ship for a consultation. They hadn't said a word when Julke had added Zade's name to the list.

Luckily, *Wobbly*'s cargo airlock was good enough to connect directly to the bigger Volksstam ship. It would have been a travesty to punch a new hole in the beautiful *Wobbly* for a new airlock.

Though he'd been tempted to take Mayek with him, he'd decided all the griffins would be safer staying on *Wobbly*. As a precaution, he'd shut them in the largest cargo hold with enough open mealpacks to keep them busy for a day. Cleaning up the mess would be a small price to pay.

As they crossed the threshold, Zade trailed the group, watching Julke. Once again, he was the noob, watching the smartest person on the ship so he could stay alive. The only difference was, this time, he didn't want to escape.

He did, however, want to clean up before meeting the grand matriarch. She clearly terrified the other Volksstam and made brave, wily Julke square her shoulders like she was marching into battle.

His exosuit stank, and he stank even worse. After six days of wearing it, with no way to clean out the pads, he felt like moss had started to grow between his toes, and less comfortable places. He'd have gladly traded his hearing protection implants for odor-blocking implants. The only consolation was that the rest of their little group smelled just as bad.

Apparently, someone anticipated this problem, because the person who greeted them took them straight to separate small rooms with their own tiny freshers. They'd even provided clothes. Zade used the chem spray cycle three times before he felt clean enough to slip into the pullover robe and belt it, then step into the loose sandals. He left the odiferous exosuit in the far corner. The room would probably have to be fumigated if they didn't get the suit out of there soon.

The door chimed, then opened to reveal Julke dressed

in a similar robe and sandals. She held out her hand. "Time for the pageant."

He took her proffered hand, glad for the contact and to briefly reconnect his empath talent with hers. If he'd been a telepath, he could have told her he'd back any play she came up with. Since he wasn't, all he could do was share his love and his determination to support her.

Once they were taken to the audience with Benthe Robynsdytr, he could see why Julke called it the pageant.

The room was big enough to rival a prosperous space trader guild hall. The decoration style could charitably be called eclectic, with a dizzying mix of art, color, and function. The twenty or so people in the hall had plenty of choices for chairs. Three giant holo displays showed groups of more people, presumably live connections to the other eight Volksstam ships that accompanied the *Ars Memoriae*.

Benthe Robynsdytr sat in the center of the room on an ornate chair. The raised dais under her had three steps on both sides and the front. Behind her, a long antique was filled with serving dishes of food. The wonderful smells had Zade's stomach reminding him that it had been shamefully neglected of late. If he never saw another prisoner mealpack containing "pasty striped neochi," whatever that was supposed to be, it would be too soon.

Blessedly, Benthe, as she'd told everyone to address her, wasted no time in cutting to the core. She greeted the other Volksstam prisoners each by name, welcoming them back and saying she was looking forward to hearing their stories. That was the gist, anyway, based on Zade's limited understanding of classical Dutch.

Then she turned to look at Julke and him. He couldn't see any physical resemblance to Julke, other than height, but she had the same force of personality.

"Julke Defayensdytr, I understand you have important news." Her Standard English had a hint of clipped consonants.

Zade hid a frown. Maybe it was just the Volksstam way, but it felt like disrespect for Benthe to be less welcoming to her own granddaughter than she was to the others. Despite his determined containment, he couldn't help but notice that the matriarch was a shielder, a miniature black hole as far as emotions. Sometimes shielders had a hard time letting other people in.

Julke let go of his hand and stepped forward. "Yes, but first, does Erteke Kraaiensdytr still lead the Judicatory Council, and is she still matriarch of her *familiestam*? And do the Kraaiens still have the largest fleet?"

"Yes, to all those questions." Benthe's raised eyebrow invited Julke to continue.

"Then perhaps my information is still of value. Five hundred days ago, I discovered the Kraaiens fleet had secret orders to attack independent traders, shipping companies, CGC military patrol ships, and frontier planets. The goal was not acquisition, but to goad the victims to break alliances and retaliate against each other. When Kraaiens discovered we'd also accidentally been sent these orders, Erteke Kraaiensdytr herself ordered Mees Kraaienszoon to kill me, or so he said. Owing to our former relationship, he instead sent me to Nova Nine recruiters. An act of mercy, he said."

Benthe's expression hardened for a split second before

smoothing into unreadable blandness. "Mees personally presented convincing evidence to the Assembly that your ship and crew were lost to an unprovoked attack by a trade guild ship." She paused. "We disbelieved their claim of innocence."

Zade suspected the diplomatic words alluded to less-diplomatic actions. The pirate clan name might be insulting, but it wasn't entirely unjustified, either. He also gathered that the Kraaiens matriarch's position on the council was significant.

"These are matters to consider later." Benthe stood. "I invited you here to commend you for forging and maintaining the prisoner alliance. And for advocating for them during negotiations t fairly dividing the bounty of the antique ships and their contents. I am extremely proud that you are my granddaughter. I also owe you an apology."

A slight murmur from the crowd suggested Benthe's words surprised them. Emotions in the room notched up, pushing against his containment.

Benthe walked to the edge of the dais, her focus on Julke. "Twenty years ago, I named you 'voyager' and sent you out to find your place in the universe. I was wrong. Now more than ever, the Volksstam need people like you to help us hold our community together in spite of adversity. And even if I discounted the stories told by the other escapees, the number of trader and frontier planet representatives who responded to your call is illuminating."

Zade wished he could see Julke's face because whatever Benthe saw made her tighten her lips. With a measured breath, she shrugged out of the embroidered calf-length vest and let it drop to the floor as she descended the steps to stand two meters from Julke.

"The news of your death devastated me. It made me realize I'd driven you away just like I'd done with the other people I loved most. Because of politics, I have been too much the matriarch and not enough the friend or the claimed. Or the grandmother. The loss of your mother and brother hit me hard, but I told myself at the time I couldn't afford to be weak."

Unexpectedly, Benthe's shield softened. Zade detected the tannin taste of remorse and the ash taste of sorrow. Reaction silently rippled through the room.

"I remember a day long ago when you stood in a hall like this, miserable in your grief, wanting me to hold you. To my shame, I refused because others were watching." She raised her arms and held them open. A tear streaked down her cheek. "Could I ask for a hug from my cherished, beloved granddaughter?"

Julke stumbled into Benthe's arms and wrapped herself around her grandmother.

A few moments later, the two women separated. Benthe wiped her face, then nodded regally at the assemblage and, with a silent wave of her hand, invited them to the food.

Zade gently invited Julke into his own arms and cradled her against him. Her tears dampened his tunic. He let the giant waves of her emotions pass over and through him. "What do you need?"

"This," she said with a sigh. "And food that doesn't come from a mealpack. And a place where we can–"

A man approached and cleared his throat. "Benthe asked me to tell you that Zade Lunaso has a ping from the Chiseko Fento Homesteaders Association." He nodded once then turned and walked away.

Julke tilted her head up to give him a questioning look.

"The frontier planet where I was going before I met you. But my claim payment was to the settlement company, not them."

"Chiseko Fento sent a defender ship to the rescue." The corner of her mouth twitched in humor. "As far as I know, it's their entire fleet." She relaxed her arms but slipped her hand in his. "Let's eat, then find a place where we can talk." With her other palm on his face, she drew him down for a quick kiss. "And other things."

FAR TOO MANY hours later for Zade's liking, they finally had full bellies, an assigned guest suite, and the promise of a few hours of privacy. And no stinking exosuits.

The small anteroom held four padded chairs and a floating desk with a comms display he'd just finished using. He went to the bedroom where Julke was seated on the bed that took up nearly the entire room, deftly braiding dark and light wavy strands of her hair. She looked up with a smile that lit her face.

"Chaos, but you're gorgeous." The words were out before he could wonder if appearance compliments pleased or irritated her. He had so much to learn about the woman he'd fallen in love with.

Her smile hadn't dimmed, so he got to the point.

"Chiseko Fento wants to register the homestead property with my name on it, and make the settlement company accept it. All I'd need to do is stay for one year to complete the claim." He gave her a crooked smile. "I can't tell if they're desperate for settlers, or want to curry favor with you, or both."

Her expression gave no hint of what she was thinking. "What do you want to do?"

In quiet moments, he'd been asking himself the same question. "I think I kept jumping from crew to crew because I was hoping for something like the family I never had. Since I wasn't finding it in the starlanes, I thought I'd have better luck on a frontier planet. Seeing what you did with the prisoners made me realize that instead of just looking, I should have been building. I'd like to build a life with you." He took a deep breath and let it out. "But not if it jeopardizes your place among your people. And other than a possible plot of land on Chiseko Fento, I have no assets, at least until I get my share from selling the antique ships." As the prisoner with the least time at Nova Nine, his share was the smallest, but even that would be more credits than he'd ever had all at once. But he wouldn't be seeing them anytime soon.

"I know what I want." She patted the bed beside her, inviting him to sit. When he did, she slipped her hand into his. "I'd claim you in a heartbeat, but that's not fair until you know what it is. So, I have a proposition. Come with me to the cityships. Learn about our culture. Meet people who will appreciate your talents and gifts as much as I do. See what claiming means."

She wrapped his hand in both of hers. "But my

grandmother wasn't wrong to call me *reiziger*, a voyager. I can only take the cityships for so long, and then I have to leave for the sake of my sanity. My point is, I'm not the only one who doesn't thrive in the confines of our conjoined ships. I'm betting we can find someone in the Volksstam who will trade valuable assets for that land. That would give you independence instead of being beholden to any Volksstam *familiestam*, including mine. Especially mine."

"Yes, please." Zade lifted their joined hands and kissed the back of hers. "Will they let us bring the griffins? I don't think Mayek or the three rock-heads will be happy without me. And Sutrio says Moonlet is pining for you."

She laughed. "The cityships will adore our griffins. If Sutrio's sanctuary and breeding program idea works out, and you act as her sales agent, you'll both have Volksstam queuing up and offering premium trades."

He lowered his mouth to hers for a languid kiss that quickly became incendiary as he felt her empath talent escaped containment to spiral sensuously with his. "How about we adore each other for a while?"

She smiled under his lips. "Yes, please."

A gentle breeze brought a whiff of fragrant *narcissi* to Julke's nose as she walked along the long corridor. Even though it has been nearly half a year since she'd returned to the cityships, the sweet scents of home still brought a smile to her face.

The arching, shades-of-gold corridor was not as popular as the shortcut tubes that had been added to the Robyn *familieschips* cluster in later years. Clever illustrations behind the linear rows of leafy vining oxy plants made the wide, gently oval shape look more like the entry to a terrapark than the hallway of a starship connector. The interspersed bright pink-and orange five-petal flowers enhanced the illusion.

It was almost hot in the warmer midday bright lighting cycle, which was part of why Julke often went that way. Her soft boots hardly made a sound on the springy surface of the walkway. Gentle breezes that helped direct dust toward the filters helped the plants thrive and offered welcome coolness — and scents — to humans.

Walking the old connector instead of taking a faster capsule gave her a much-needed decompression between her grandmother's increasingly complex business meetings and her quiet time at home. It reminded her of the long access tunnels in her mother's biggest *familieschip* that snaked between engines and enviro systems. Running through them at top speed had given her the illusion of freedom.

Adulthood had brought actual freedom, not counting her five hundred days in Nova Nine. But freedom also brought obligations to her family and the Volksstam. Travelers like her were agents of change and often resented for it. Unfortunately for the traditionalists, the gods of Chaos liked kicking up storms, whether her people were ready or not.

But freedom also brought blessings, like the snoozing griffin resting on her shoulder pad. Her feathery tail wrapped down across Julke's back and waist like a sash. Moonlet didn't like tense meetings any more than Julke did. Neither of them could completely block heated emotions in a room full of competitive people in high-stakes negotiations.

And thank all the gods of Chaos for the blessing that was Zade Lunaso.

She was both amazed and amused at how well the man — and his griffins — fit in with the Volksstam way of life. He'd built a successful venture in an unfamiliar community and made more friends than enemies. It helped that he freely shared his wealth of knowledge about Central Galactic Concordance ship design and operation with Volksstamers who had a mutual interest.

And as her politically savvy grandmother Benthe slyly pointed out, he and the five other ex-Nova Nine prisoners who'd been granted sponsorship in the cityships served another purpose. They were living proof that the CGC produced good people, and not just the ignorant, lazy *slakken* that more bigoted Volksstam believed.

Moonlet roused on her shoulder to look up at the upcoming intersection. Julke felt the edges of aura signatures she recognized. She'd gotten into the habit of always checking, even close to home. The disgraced Kraiien family had lost power, but even after paying heavy damages, they'd still have more than enough credits to richly reward anyone who made her disappear again, this time for good.

She briefly patted her darling griffin's tail end. "Not all humans have treats, *lieveling*."

Zade had cleverly taught his personal griffins to alert on strangers, but he'd failed with Moonlet. She was too fond of people to see them as potential enemies.

Julke exchanged polite nods with the two Volksstamers who passed by, then picked up her pace. Seeing the savory pastry in the one man's hand reminded her that Zade had promised her a fine midday meal. She laughed at herself as she took the turn toward home. She was becoming as food-motivated as a certain darling little griffin.

After she greeted Zade with a kiss and coaxed Moonlet into an open cage, she kicked off her boots and followed Zade through the long, narrow kitchen to the dining area.

Technically, it was a galley, but the tiny personal ship she'd inherited from her mother and brother hadn't been detached from the *familieschip* cluster since before she was born. It was big enough for two humans, but five airborne griffins could make it feel like living in a care center for thrill-seeking toddlers.

"This is amazing." Julke marveled at how many dishes Zade had managed to fit on their small table and still have room for plates and utensils. "Have you been training the *Planeten* to help with cooking?" She counted six different foods, and all of them her favorites.

"Chaos, no." Zade laughed as he put his arm around her waist. "I had to bribe them just to stay out of the kitchen while I practiced." He tilted his head up toward the high recessed ceiling ledge where the three pale rock griffins named for the planets Mercury, Jupiter, and Neptune now dozed. "Out of fairness, I had to bribe Mayek, too, and now he's too plump to be stealthy."

Chucking, she gave him a kiss. "Thank you for this. It looks too pretty to touch, except I'm starving."

"Good." He waved her toward a chair. "That velvet box on the plate is for you."

She threw him a puzzled glance, then stepped closer to pick it up. Lifting the hinged lid revealed an exquisitely detailed metal-printed pendant of Moonlet on a filigreed chain.

Zade bowed respectfully to her. "Julke Defayensdytr, I was wondering if your heart and affections are being appreciated. Because if not, I'd like to claim them."

Surprise made her blink. He had to have been

planning this for weeks. Somehow, he'd managed to hide his intentions, despite how much they talked about everything.

She couldn't help but grin. "Depends. I'm looking for a fair trade. Are your heart and affections available for claiming?"

He nodded solemnly. "As long as you're making the claim, they are." The intensity of his gaze made her heart skip a beat.

"Then I'll take that trade, Zade Lunaso." She bowed briefly, then held out her hand to him and let her empath talent loose to twirl with his. "I love you."

The joy on his face matched his emotions as he reeled her in for a long, sensuous kiss. "I adore you."

Her stomach growled, making her laugh.

He pulled back a little. "Sorry, I probably should have waited until after you ate, but you're too smart, and I wanted to surprise you."

Reaching up, she smoothed the loose lock of hair back behind his ear. "You did." It was the truth. Family drama had kept her in crisis reaction mode instead of planning mode, where she preferred to be.

"Good. Let's eat so we have time for a nap." He smiled with wolfish interest. "And other forms of relaxation."

"Oh, yes." She gave him one last kiss before separating. "Lots of relaxation."

Julke couldn't remember a time when she'd been happier. Good food, good company, and a claimed who loved her as much as she loved him. Not to mention he was supernova hot, in and out of bed.

She set the two glasses of chilled tea she carried on the bedside shelf, taking advantage of the angle to admire the muscled curve of his hip and thigh. Unable to resist, she slid across the resilk sheet to snug herself against him, head on his shoulder and arm across his chest. Skin to skin contact stirred her talent. Her body might be sated, but she'd never tire of the subtle dance of their talents.

"Thank you." He kissed her hair. "Do we have to announce our claims somewhere?"

She loved that he'd taken the time to research the text variations and chosen the best one for them. "Depends. Old style, we'd make a public scene in some crowded venue. My great grandmother pickpocketed her target in broad daylight and demanded a claim if he wanted the goods returned. He threatened to shoot her if she didn't accept his claim."

A wave of alarm crossed his emotional sea. "What's the new style?"

She lifted herself briefly to kiss his jawline. "We tell a few friends. Everyone else will figure it out, eventually. Kind of like on Nova Nine, when we all knew which guards were hot-connecting with which staff or when relationships crashed."

"I like new style." His arm wrapped around her shoulders. "Nova Nine tanked on every level, but it brought me to you. I'd be dead without you." He smiled. "I hardly ever get mistaken for one of the *beschaafd* anymore. Until my 'civilized' new Dutch gets me in trouble with older classical Dutch speakers."

"You rekindled my hope." Closing her eyes, she breathed in the scent of him. "We're good for each other. Like when you help anchor me when the bad dreams try to drag me into hellspace." She'd tried working with the Volksstam therapists to help with post-trauma damage, but none of them knew what to do for her, and even less so for telepath-immune Zade. His empath talent held her tight, and she used hers to soothe his wounds.

Seeing the need, they'd organized a survivor's group of the Volksstam returnees and the others who'd been granted asylum. Only other Nova Nine prisoners really understood. The members still talked, though not as regularly as they had the first few ten-days after the rescue.

And despite having only a private hypothesis, she was convinced that they'd all been helped by the griffins. She and Zade knew Sutrio was right about them being empathic. Not all the ex-prisoners believed that, but caring for their personal griffins gave them positive experiences to remember.

That reminded her of another matter. "Did you read this morning's message from Sutrio?" She rolled up and reached for the tea glasses, holding one for him as he sat up.

"Yes." He slid back to rest against the padded wall, his knees raised. "She doesn't strike me as the type to ask for help unless she needs it."

"I agree." She gave him his glass, then faced him, sitting cross-legged. "Trouble is, I have to be here until the final judgment is ratified, which is at least another ten-day." She blew out a frustrated sigh. "If I leave now, the Kraiiens will convince everyone I was lying, or part of a conspiracy, or something else twisty. To be honest, I don't care as much about the reparations they owe me and my family as I do about leaving them free to sow their poisonous brand of discord and strife throughout the known galaxy. 'Enhanced revenue opportunities for all,' my ass."

"I've avoided politics like griffins avoid baths, but I hear things. Kraiiens are worse than jackers when it comes to business deals. At least jackers will rob you up front." A frown settled on his face. "Speaking of which, with Captain Fazhian still offering a high bounty for me, even if I had funds for a ship, I couldn't visit Sutrio without a new identity and heavy security."

"Plus, your security would need trade experience and makeovers at the nearest body parlor, or the CGC military would detain them for being 'pirate clan piranhas.'" She reached out to pat his thigh. "You, they'd detain because you're so plasma hot."

A delighted grin lit up his face. "Thank you. Whatever delusion drug you're putting in the tea, keep drinking it."

"You're welcome." He was easy to please. She suspected he'd been deprived of compliments before they met, so she'd been trying to make up for it. "The Robyn family council approved Prughal's full adoption this morning. They are now officially Prughal Robynmensen."

"Good." He sipped his tea. "They're thriving here. They deserve a secure home."

"They do." She didn't know the details, but Prughal's aura had layers of tragedy that were far older than his Nova Nine experience. The Volksstam embraced non-binary people, but she suspected the *beschaafd* parts of the CGC couldn't say the same. "Benthe is priming them to consult for enviro systems and hydroponics. Their plant affinity is a very valuable talent. We Volksstamers depend on well-run ships to sustain life."

"Everyone deserves the chance to do what they're good at." A thoughtful look crossed his face. "I know *familiestams* are sort of like businesses, but yet not. Can they... I don't know the right words. Get bought out?"

"They can merge and blend the lineages. Or they can register an alliance. Smaller families with assets like rich trade routes or good minder talents can get protection from bigger families. If a family has more liabilities than assets, the debt holders can band together and can force a merger." She frowned. "That's a recent trend. Big, prosperous families are acting too much like civilized mega-corps that make money for money's sake, rather than looking out for the people. Kraiiens are the worst, but they're not alone."

His thoughtful look deepened. "Should the rest of us from the CGC be looking for families to adopt us so we're safe, too?"

She hadn't considered it from that angle before, and she should have. "I don't think I'm the right person to ask. Travelers like me don't have our fingers on the pulse of current Volksstam society. But I'm not sure I'd ask Benthe, either. She's trying hard to be a better family heart, but she still sees everything through the lens of politics."

His foot turned to touch her knee. "Do you have to be anywhere this afternoon?"

She shook her head. "I took the rest of the day off. The negotiations have been a hell of a ride."

"I'm worried about your stress levels. I remember what

you said about the cityships making you crazy." He cradled the glass in his hands. "I'm worried you're staying here longer than you wanted to because of me and the griffin enterprise."

"I'd have been stuck here for the adjudication, regardless." She put her glass back on the shelf, then scooted closer to him. "You give me the patience to see it through. I've got an idea for what to do with the reparations funds."

"I love your plans." He patted her thigh with his slightly chilly hand. "Tell me about this one."

She took a deep breath. "Buy a bigger, faster ship and convince Benthe to fund a crew. I want a formal commission to repair the damage done by the Kraiiens by rebuilding and solidifying the alliances between the traders and frontier planets that came to our rescue." She hadn't said it out loud before, but it felt right when she did. Zade was so easy to talk to.

"I'm in." His warm smile faded to a more serious expression. "I remember what you said about helping innocent people when the galaxy burns. If I can spend my life doing that with you, I would consider myself truly blessed." He took a large gulp of his tea, emptying the glass. "I've got sales contracts out for the last three griffins. Can we visit Sutrio... damn. She needs help sooner than we can get there."

Something he'd said earlier bubbled up in her mind. "I wonder if Pim might be available."

"Pim?" His tone invited her to explain.

"You know him as Berend Okaansson, the translator

for your griffin sales contracts. His friends call him Pim. I grew up with him. He's got a couple of decades of trade experience and his own solo ship, but his family won't let him use it. They keep him in the back office as a glorified porter."

Zade nodded. "I remember him. Tall for a Volksstamer. The griffins liked him as much as he liked them." He rubbed one eye. "What's the malfunction with his family?"

"They're living in the past. They adopted a very talented outsider a few generations back, but they tank at business. They're too proud to admit they can't afford to operate their crewed ships anymore." She made a rude sound. "But I'll bet they'd take a commission from the Robyn family right now. They hate the Kraiiens."

"Let's ask him. I'll help pay that commission." He turned to her. "How about this? I get my new Volksstam friends who love ships to show me theirs, and ask about likely candidates for sale. I'll check with Lantham, too. You slice-and-haul every credit you can out of Kraiiens, then convince Benthe we've been charged by gods of Chaos for a galactic peace and harmony mission. Our first stop will be the griffin sanctuary to see how Sutrio is doing."

"You're good at plans, too." Until she met him, she'd never realized what a difference a positively adventurous partner made in her life.

"You'll have to help me with a new identity that'll pass CGC authentication. They've gotten less lazy about checking these days. And maybe a bodyshop visit, too." He ran a hand over the lightning pattern sculpted into the side of his short, dark hair. "A Volksstam style won't fool grudge-holding captains who still want me for vengeance."

"She can't have you." Julke pulled him in for a firm, possessive kiss. "You're mine, and I'm keeping you."

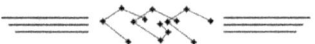

ABOUT THE BOOK

Thanks for reading *Escape from Nova Nine*. I love stories with unlikely heroes who take long-shot chances to be together and save their world, even if it's just an asteroid. The griffins were inspired by my veterinarian friend's clever and mischievous parrot.

If you love space opera, adventure, and romance, check out OVERLOAD FLUX. Two misfits have secrets they must keep. But if they expose the secrets of a corrupt pharma corp, they may end up dead.

A shorter version of *Escape from Nova Nine* debuted in the *Pets in Space 6* science fiction romance anthology. Profits from the Pets in Space® anthologies support Hero-Dogs.org, a charity that provides trained support dogs to disabled U.S. veterans and first-responders to improve their quality of life.

When the cure for a deadly disease is stolen, two misfits are all that stands between greed and intergalactic tragedy.

Luka Foxe can't let anyone know about his secret mental abilities. Debilitated by their influence when faced with violence, the brilliant forensic investigator now only takes assignments involving theft. But when he has to hunt down a hijacked vaccine for a galaxy-wide pandemic, the tragic first clue is his best friend's brutal murder.

Nightshift guard Mairwen Morganthur knows she must keep a low profile. The product of illegal genetic alteration, she's a lethal weapon with no social graces. But when she's tasked to protect a detective with frightening intuition, she finds herself falling for him even though he could expose her.

Racing to recover the cure for a galaxy-wide pandemic, Luka is surprised by his developing feelings for the capable-but-mysterious guard. And Mairwen may have to risk everything by revealing her identity, with deadly mercenaries hot on their tail.

Can the unlikely pair survive an interplanetary conspiracy long enough to save lives and find love?

Overload Flux is the first novel in the sweeping Central Galactic Concordance space opera series. If you like haunted characters, compelling mysteries, and interstellar romance, then you'll enjoy Carol Van Natta's epic tale.

**Buy Overload Flux to uncover
cosmic corruption today!**

Author.CarolVanNatta.com/OF

*

ABOUT THE AUTHOR

Carol Van Natta is a USA TODAY bestselling science fiction and fantasy author. Works include the award-winning Central Galactic Concordance space opera series and the Ice Age Shifters® paranormal romance series. In addition, she edits the Pets in Space science fiction romance anthology.

She shares her Colorado home with just the right number of eccentric cats. Connect with her on the web at Author.CarolVanNatta.com.